Faking It

NEW YORK TIMES BESTSELLING AUTHORS
CARLY PHILLIPS
ERIKA WILDE

New York Times Bestselling Authors Carly Phillips and
Erika Wilde bring you a new fun, flirty, standalone romance.

Confirmed bachelor Max Sterling isn't into rescuing damsels
in distress, but when the very tempting Hailey Ellison needs
his help, there's only one thing for him to do. Step in and
pose as her loving fiancé. Except there is nothing fake about
his attraction to her, or how much he wants her beneath
him in his bed, moaning his name. But what starts as a sexy,
flirty, temporary engagement, quickly becomes something
more serious that neither one ever anticipated.

* * *

Chapter One

As Hailey Ellison crossed the street toward her eleven-thirty appointment, she decided it should be against every rule in the universe for a man to be as devastatingly gorgeous as Max Sterling. Why? Because it just wasn't fair to expect any woman to have to function professionally in his presence when all she really wanted to do was swoon at his sheer masculinity.

She approached the man in question, whose attention was on his phone as he typed out either an email or a text, a troublesome frown furrowing his brow. But even a scowl on his handsome face couldn't detract from the butterflies suddenly taking flight in her stomach. And lucky her . . . the fact that he was otherwise distracted at the moment gave her the opportunity to admire him for a few extra seconds.

No hardship there, she thought with a dreamy sigh.

As a top-notch luxury real estate broker in Chicago, and her agent of three months, Max always looked the part and dressed to impress—tailored suits, designer shoes, and silk ties. She'd never seen him in anything other than business attire, but even as impeccable and well put together as he always looked, his dark brown hair was perpetually a tousled mess, which only added to his attractiveness, along with that glimmer of bad-boy charm he exuded. His lips were full and sensual and quick to smile—unlike at the moment—and those mesmerizing hazel eyes of his never ceased to make her weak-kneed and tongue-tied.

For an average, ordinary-looking woman like her, sexy and sophisticated Max Sterling was way out of her league and nothing more than an enjoyable fantasy she indulged in way too often. He'd never given her any indication of interest in her other than as his client, had never overtly flirted with her, and was always the epitome of a gentleman whenever they were together. Over the past three months, they'd established an easy, comfortable business relationship, and no inappropriate lines had ever been crossed—physically or verbally.

Then again, there was no reason for him to behave any differently toward her, especially when he believed she was engaged to someone else—a fabrication she perpetuated for both business and personal reasons. The day they'd met for the first time at his Premier Realty office, he'd noticed the diamond solitaire on her left-hand ring finger. He'd been quick to congratulate her on her upcoming nuptials and had treated her with nothing but respect ever since.

She'd been relegated to the friend zone, which kind of sucked, because Max Sterling was the first man in a long time who made her regret wearing a ring on her finger, and her reasons for it being there. Every time they were together, he made her wish that she was more sexually confident and felt less inadequate when it came to her body image. Beneath the size-fourteen clothing she now wore was still that insecure fat girl who'd been ridiculed for her weight for most of her life. The chubby teenager who'd been told more times than she could count that she had such a pretty face and gorgeous hair, and it was such a shame that she was so heavy. That same girl who'd given her virginity to the first guy she'd dated in college after losing over seventy pounds, only to have him end their short-lived relationship the next day over one single, devastating text: *I'm sorry, but I'm just not into fat chicks.*

That incident had put a stranglehold on her confidence, and even now, at the age of twenty-six, those cruel words still haunted her. Of course, she'd gone out with other men since then, but that fear and distrust were always lingering in the back of her mind, forcing her to relive that humiliating incident and reminding her just how imperfect she truly was.

She didn't have to pay a therapist for her to realize that those deeply rooted self-doubts were the impetus for why she managed to sabotage every relationship she'd had since college before anything intimate developed. It was purely a defense mechanism to protect her heart and emotions, and six months ago, after breaking things off with the man she'd been dating because he'd wanted more sexually, she'd decided that, for now, it was best if she kept her focus on growing her company to the next level, because men, and her insecurities, only made the entire mix more complicated.

She'd never been in love, and yes, she was painfully aware of what a contradiction that was considering she made a living as a professional matchmaker. She had a stellar reputation for being one of the best dating services in Chicago for the wealthy and affluent. She might not have found love for herself, but she was damn good at matching others. Her success rate was nearly ninety percent, and that credibility along with word of mouth had her business, the Ellison Agency, booming.

Which was why she was in the market for just the right piece of property to purchase so she could expand beyond the cramped office space she'd been using for the past four years. Max had shown her at least a dozen places over a three-month period, but so far, she'd yet to find *the one*, and she refused to settle for anything less than the dream office building she envisioned.

Yes, she was being incredibly specific and particular, and with each listing Max presented and she rejected, she kept expecting him to give up on her out of sheer frustration. To write her off as difficult and demanding and decide to cut her loose as a client before she wasted any more of his time. It was a familiar pattern with her when it came to guys in general, and that cautious part of her psyche figured that this situation with Max wouldn't be much different, and it was just a matter of time before he gave up on her.

Yet . . . he'd remained patient and persistent in his quest to find that elusive piece of property she'd described to him. Despite how many listings he'd shown her, she never felt pressured to buy, nor had she been made to feel that she was a pain in the ass. He genuinely seemed to care about what she wanted and needed, which made her wonder if he was just as indulgent and determined in the bedroom when it came to a woman's pleasure . . .

Just as that arousing thought crossed her mind and a small, unexpected moan of longing tickled the back of her throat—a sound that had obviously alerted him to the fact that he was no longer alone—he shifted his attention from his phone and glanced up. She was probably ten paces away, and as soon as he saw her, that aggravating frown that had creased his brows just seconds ago diminished, and one of those sexy, thigh-clenching smiles curved his lips.

On cue, her heart rate increased and her legs

turned to jelly.

His direct gaze met hers, his warm, hazel eyes more green than brown today. But no matter the color, when they were trained so intently on her, so warm and spellbinding, she had to remind herself to *breathe*.

Inhaling deeply, she tamped down her attraction to him so she didn't do or say something foolish, and when she was finally standing beside him, she returned his smile.

"Hi, Max." At least she managed to sound composed and business-like.

Now that they were on a friendlier basis, they no longer shook hands, which she secretly missed. It had been her one valid excuse to touch him, to feel his long fingers sliding along her palm so sensually before engulfing her hand in the warmth of his. He had nice, big, strong hands, and . . . she really needed to reign in her misbehaving thoughts.

"Hi, Hailey. I know this was a last-minute call, but I'm glad you could make it," he said, his smooth, naturally seductive voice causing the tips of her breasts to tighten and rasp against the lace lining of her bra.

Stupid, traitorous nipples. She didn't have to look down to know they were making themselves known against her blouse, like two twin hussies trying to get Max's attention. She was grateful that he wasn't one of those kinds of guys who would deliberately look and smirk. No, Mr. Sterling had impeccable manners when he was around her. Hell, he'd probably never even noticed that she *had* breasts, or most likely, he just didn't care because she wasn't his type. Even better, since she was *engaged*, she reminded herself.

"You sounded excited about this listing," she said, glancing up at the exterior of the contemporary-looking building they were standing in front of—a three-story chrome-and-glass structure in the trendy Logan Square. The location was a quick twenty-minute drive from downtown Chicago, which also meant she'd get more building for her buck outside of the city limits.

"A friend of mine is looking to put this building on the market, and I immediately thought of you." Dark green eyes sparkled with an enthusiasm that was infectious. "In fact, I'm so confident that it's going to come damn close to checking off every box on that wish list of yours that I didn't even list the property because I wanted to make sure you had first crack at it."

Yes, she had a wish list. If she was going to spend a high six figures on a place of business, then it needed to meet every one of her requirements and then some. "No one else has seen the place?"

He shook his head. "Nope. Trust me, Hailey, this property has your name written all over it, and I wasn't about to let anyone else near this building until you looked it over first."

She laughed, even though she appreciated just how diligent he was about finding her a building that fulfilled her expectations. "I'm thinking you're hoping I'll jump on it so you won't have to deal with the most demanding, pain-in-the-ass client in all of Chicago for another three months."

"Not even close," he said, amusement infusing his always upbeat voice. "You're far from difficult. You know what you want, and I happen to like a decisive woman. It was just a matter of being patient and waiting until the right piece of property came on the market. I think today is going to be your lucky day."

He was so sure of himself, and she tipped her head to the side, causing her long, wavy blonde hair to tumble over her right shoulder. "You really think so, huh?"

"I *know* so," he said, and winked at her.

Of course, it wasn't a *flirtatious* wink, but that didn't stop her pulse from skipping a beat and those butterflies from swirling in her stomach again.

The phone in his hand pinged, and he glanced at the lit-up display, that perturbed frown appearing again.

"Everything okay?" she asked. "I don't mind waiting if you have something you need to attend to."

He shook his head and looked back at her with a smile that didn't completely erase the slight furrow between his brows. "Sorry. It's nothing important. Let's head inside so you can check out the place."

He tucked his phone into the inside breast pocket of his suit jacket so she had his undivided attention, and they walked side by side up to the glass door leading into the bottom level of the building. He unlocked the door and held it open for her, and she slipped past him, catching the enticing fragrance of his cologne that never failed to arouse every one of her senses. It was warm and sensual but subtle, like black silk wrapped in masculine heat. The smell of him was like an addicting pheromone, and it took major restraint on her part not to rub up against him like a kitten rolling in catnip and bury her face against his neck for a long, deep inhale of his male essence.

The door closed behind them, and he flipped a switch on the nearby wall that turned on the lights affixed to the steel beams above them. They were standing in the lobby, which opened up into a spacious reception area that would easily fit two couches, end tables, and a few chairs. The walls were a soft gray hue, with plank flooring in a complementary slate color that gave the place a modern vibe.

At first glance, she really liked what she saw, but she also knew that was subject to change as the rest of the building's layout was revealed. It wouldn't be the first time a listing started out with promise and ended with disappointment, so she kept her initial reaction to herself.

"So, this first floor is pretty much set up and ready to go for commercial use," Max told her as he led the way down a wide hallway, drawing her attention to one of the open doors with a wave of his hand. "There are three separate rooms with built-in workstations and shelving, which would be great for individual offices, a conference room, or whatever else you might need."

She peeked inside one of the rooms, impressed with how large they were and especially appreciating the expanse of windows along the side wall that allowed natural light to filter into the first floor of the building. She really only needed two offices. One for herself and one for Brielle, her best friend and right-hand woman at the Ellison Agency, but she did like the idea of having a separate room for meetings with clients.

They reached the end of the hallway and Max pointed to the right. "There's an elevator that goes to all three floors, but you do need a key to get to the third floor, which is a two-bedroom, two-bathroom apartment."

She came to an abrupt stop beside him and gasped in shock. "Did you just say *apartment?*" One of the things on her wish list was an attached residence, which had been nonexistent up to this listing. She'd pretty much given up hope on finding a building with that particular feature.

A sexy smirk curved his lips, and his eyes gleamed with wicked delight. "Ahh, you caught that, did you?"

He seemed very pleased with himself, and

she was giddy with the possibility that this place might be *the one*, just as Max had promised.

He inclined his head, his gorgeous features completely dazzling her. "Come on. I'm not done wowing you just yet."

Instead of taking the elevator, they ascended the open staircase to the second floor, and Hailey's breath caught in her throat as she assessed the open concept of the room in front of her that was beyond perfect for the reception and mixer parties she held for her clients. The chrome embellishments and fixtures against the gray walls provided a sophisticated yet elegant atmosphere that she instantly fell in love with.

The sitting and lounge area was huge, with plenty of space for mingling, as well as places for private conversations between couples. A full bar for serving cocktails encompassed an entire wall, and as they walked toward the back of the room, Max showed her the small kitchen for the caterers she hired to use.

With her speechless and in awe, he led the way to the elevator, and once they were inside, he inserted the key so that there were delivered to the third floor. The doors opened directly into an apartment that was bigger and more luxurious than the current one she was living in, and by the time Max was done showing her the entire upstairs, she was giddy and nearly bursting with exhilaration.

There was only one thing keeping her from expressing her elation and shouting *I'll take it!*, and that was the cost. A move-in-ready place like this couldn't be cheap, but it was exactly what she needed to take the Ellison Agency to the next level.

Back in the apartment living room, she turned to face Max, who was watching her expectantly, clearly waiting for her reaction—and obviously expecting an exuberant one. It was all she could do to keep from bouncing on the balls of her feet. No way was she giving in to premature excitement until she had all the details to make an informed decision.

She shifted anxiously on her feet. "I'm afraid to ask the price on this building."

"Hailey," he said softly, cajolingly, his voice sounding husky to her ears—or maybe she just imagined it. "Didn't I tell you to trust me before we even entered the building? I wouldn't bring you to a property that wasn't within your budget."

She bit her bottom lip, and for a brief moment, his gaze lowered to her mouth, then quickly returned to her face. "Don't tease me, Max."

Now whose voice was husky? *Hers, that's who.* And as for the *don't tease me* reply, its purpose was twofold. One, she really wanted to believe this amazing place could possibly be hers, so she prayed that he wasn't pulling her leg. And two, having his eyes on her mouth, even for a quick, limited time that probably meant nothing to him, was the epitome of being teased with something she'd never have or experience... feeling his lips sliding slowly, sensually against hers.

"I wouldn't joke about something as important as this," he assured her, and there was no refuting the sincerity in his tone. "Here's the deal. My friend is getting a divorce and wants to unload this property as quickly as possible. I ran the top end of your budget by him this morning, before even calling you to see the place, and he's already agreed to the price. This building is yours if you want it."

She absently turned the engagement ring on her finger around and around, trying to process what Max had just said. She took a moment to let his words sink in and to absorb everything that was within her grasp. She'd started her matchmaking company four years ago and had slowly built it into a reputable business that was steadily growing. She was fortunate enough to be able to do something she excelled at and enjoyed, that brought other people happiness, and equally lucky that she had a substantial trust fund left to her by her deceased parents that enabled her to avoid having to work a dreaded nine-to-five job. It was something she didn't take for granted, because given the choice, she'd choose having her mother and father alive over any amount of money.

But with each milestone she achieved, she did so knowing that her parents would be proud of her. She glanced around the apartment, resisting the urge to do a happy dance right there in front of Max. Instead, she met his confident, waiting gaze and somehow managed to remain calm and composed, like the poised businesswoman she was. Or tried to be, anyway.

"Yes," she said, her steady tone belying the jumble of emotions rising within her. "I'll take it."

"I *knew* it." A wide, brilliant grin appeared on his full lips, and he executed a triumphant fist pump, clearly proud of himself for accomplishing the challenging task of *finally* finding her a new place of business that included every feature she'd asked for.

He looked so satisfied with himself she couldn't contain the amused laughter that escaped her.

"Let me make a quick call to confirm the deal with the seller." He retrieved his phone from his suit jacket, unlocked the screen, and paused for a moment as his gaze seemed to scan something on the display.

Another annoying message, she assumed, judging by the slight clenching of his jaw before he shook his head and continued swiping through his phone. Once he had his friend's number pulled up, he connected the call and brought the device to his ear.

As soon as Max started talking to the owner of the building, she glanced away from his too captivating stare and tuned out the conversation, still afraid to get her hopes up. Instead, she started twirling the engagement ring on her finger again—something that had become a nervous habit since she'd put on the piece of jewelry. Maybe because self-consciously she knew the ring didn't really belong there, and a part of her felt bad executing the charade because she wasn't prone to lying.

But the appearance of having a fake fiancé wasn't hurting anyone, she'd reasoned with herself. And if it made her feel more secure and confident, and being in love gave credence to her expertise as a matchmaker, then the perception was like any other marketing tool, right?

"Hailey?"

She was so lost in her thoughts that she hadn't heard Max end the call. With her stomach flip-flopping with equal measures of anxiety and hope—because her chances of finding another place like this were slim to none if the owner had changed his mind for any reason—she met Max's unreadable expression.

She swallowed hard. "Yes?"

"The place is yours." A huge, delighted grin spread across his gorgeous face. "I'll submit a formal offer this afternoon and get all the paperwork in order and started. The owner asked for a thirty-day escrow, if possible, and since you're already pre-approved and offering a fifty percent cash down payment, I don't see that as an issue. In about a month, this place will belong to you and the Ellison Agency."

Ahhh. Hailey finally gave free reign to the overwhelming excitement and emotion she hadn't allowed to surface until now. Everything she'd suppressed bubbled up and burst through her in an adrenaline rush of gratitude that prompted her body to react before her brain could process her spontaneous reaction.

She flung herself against Max's chest, wrapped her arms around his neck, and hugged him tight. And she certainly didn't anticipate the next words that impulsively blurted out of her mouth. "Oh, my God, Max! I *love* you."

The hard body pressed so intimately against hers immediately stiffened, and his hands came to rest on her hips to tactfully push her away. Her inappropriate behavior along with the way Max was trying to gently but firmly put distance between them hit her like a dousing of cold water.

She quickly extricated her arms from around Max's neck and took a substantial step back so that his hands dropped from her hips. Her face heated with mortification as she tried to explain what she meant.

"I don't mean *I love you* I love you," she rambled, her embarrassment making her voice pitch higher than normal. "I meant, I love you as in you're the best real estate broker ever."

The corner of his mouth quirked with humor, though his eyes were a few shades darker than they'd been before she'd assaulted him with her hug. "I know I'm an extremely loveable guy, but I knew how you meant it," he teased.

Relief made her relax somewhat, but it didn't completely chase away the buzz of awareness still lingering from being molded against the hot, sexy man she'd been lusting over the past three months. A man who'd clearly been uncomfortable with the close proximity of her body against his a few moments ago.

She regained her composure and returned her attention to the building that was soon to be hers. "Thank you, Max," she said more calmly. "This place is everything I wanted and so much more."

"I kinda told you so." His eyes crinkled at the corners with amusement and satisfaction.

"Yes, you did." She laughed, grateful that things were back to normal between them after that awkward encounter.

He glanced at his wristwatch, then back at her with a smile. "It's too early to drink, so how about I take you to lunch to celebrate? There's a fantastic restaurant within walking distance of Premier Realty, and afterward you can come up to my office and we'll get the offer drawn up, signed, and submitted."

She nodded. "That sounds great."

As they left the building, there was only one thing that put a damper on Hailey's great mood—the realization that now that she'd found a place, there wouldn't be any other reason or excuse to see Max anymore.

Chapter Two

MAX WAS GOING straight to hell for lusting after another man's fiancée. He was absolutely sure of it.

As he followed Hailey out of the three-story building she was about to purchase, he berated himself for allowing his attraction to this *engaged* woman to obliterate any self-control he'd had over his physical response to her. Just because he'd had her soft, curvy body pressed intimately against his a few minutes ago—okay, *plastered* against him would be a more apt description—it was no excuse for his unruly dick to leap to immediate attention.

Yeah, bad choice of words, but *leap* it had, *without* his goddamn permission and before he could fully process what was happening—

beyond the instantaneous knowledge that Hailey Ellison fit against his body as if she'd been created specifically for him to fuck. In a matter of seconds, the surge of heat and awareness brought on by having her full, lush breasts crushing against his chest and her hips aligned so perfectly to his had his cock perking up and responding to all that physical stimulation.

God, he was such an asshole. It wasn't enough that he'd gotten a boner, but in that brief moment, he'd imagined what it would be like to take the embrace one or two steps further. To back her up against the nearest wall and slide one hand beneath the hem of her prim and proper black skirt that hugged her hips and flared out around her knees. To wrap that thick, silky-looking hair of hers around his other fist to pull her head back so his mouth would have unobstructed access to the creamy expanse of her throat while his fingers slipped beneath the edge of her panties and touched her intimately, deeply.

See? He was totally going to hell.

Regretfully, and out of respect, he'd pushed her away. Because it was the right thing to do, and the last thing he wanted was for her to realize his dick was hard. But mostly, he'd ended the embrace—no matter how innocent *she'd* believed the gesture was—because he had absolutely no business coveting another man's fiancée.

Yet, as she walked a few steps ahead of him, his disobedient gaze strayed from all that luxurious hair tumbling down her back and traced along the indentation of her waist. He shamelessly watched the mesmerizing sway of her hips, the perfect curve of her ass that made his palms itch to grab, caress, and smack just hard enough to make her gasp, then moan . . .

Jesus Christ, he thought with a firm shake of his head. What was he? A goddamn hormonal teenager who had no discipline when it came to a girl he was attracted to? It certainly *felt* that way, and he needed to get his shit together, like *now*.

He deliberately picked up his pace so that he was now walking by Hailey's side, and the temptation to leer at her ass was no longer an option. "When you get to Premier Realty, go ahead and park in the underground structure and I'll meet you in front of the building," he told her. "We can walk to the restaurant from there."

She glanced up at him with a smile that reflected her current happy mood—one he liked being directly responsible for. "Sounds like a plan."

They each got into their vehicles, and on the drive to the office, Max made a call to his secretary, Olivia. He gave her all the details, stipulations, and contingencies of Hailey's offer on the property so that after lunch she could read over the purchase agreement and make any changes before she signed the paperwork and he submitted the formal offer. He also asked Olivia to make a reservation at Spiaggia Cafe. The five-star restaurant was packed at lunch, but Max frequented the establishment often enough with clients that the manager always found a spot for him.

When he reached Premier Realty, he parked his Range Rover in his designated spot and met up with Hailey. Ten minutes later, they were seated at a table at Spiaggia. They each ordered lunch from the menu of Italian fare, and Max requested a bottle of Prosecco to celebrate. As soon as the waitress delivered the bubbly white wine and poured two glasses, Max lifted his toward Hailey.

"I believe congratulations are in order," he said, inclining his head as they tapped their crystal stemware together.

She took a small sip, her bright blue eyes sparkling over the rim of her drink. "I haven't signed anything yet. I'd hate to jinx the deal."

"Not going to happen," he promised, setting his glass down just as his cell phone pinged with a text message.

He'd set the device on the table, only because he never knew when he'd get an important call from a client. He also liked being available if his partner, Wes, needed to ask him a quick question about a listing. But as soon as he unlocked the screen and saw who the message was from, he swore in frustration—and aggravation—before he could stop himself. It was a gut reaction to the name mocking him on the display. Addison Brooks, a woman he'd briefly dated—mostly as a favor to his mother—and who was quickly becoming the bane of his existence. A thorn in his side. A burr beneath his saddle. And any other metaphor that applied.

"Is everything okay, Max?" Hailey asked with quiet concern. "If you need to be somewhere else, I completely understand."

It wasn't the first time today that Hailey had witnessed, and commented on, his shift in mood after a text, and it annoyed him even more that Addison had the power to interfere in his daily life and affect his normally easygoing disposition. He also realized that Hailey was giving him an easy out if he needed one, but he wasn't about to let Addison ruin this celebratory lunch with his client.

He cleared the display on his phone and shifted his attention back to the woman sitting across from him, who was the antithesis of the high-maintenance one who was starting to get on his last nerve. "I swear I'm fine."

She raised a skeptical brow. "I would bet the property I'm about to buy that you're lying," she said, calling him out in a teasing tone.

He scrubbed a hand along his jaw and blew out a long breath to ease the tension that had settled across his shoulders. "Okay, maybe I am fibbing. Just a little," he admitted with a small laugh.

The situation with Addison was beginning to stress him out, and he wasn't sure how to get the persistent woman to back off without being blatantly rude, which wasn't his style at all. He was a nice guy, but being polite wasn't working. Unfortunately, he was caught between a jagged rock and a hard place with Addison, and he had to tread carefully so he didn't end up causing a rift between two influential business associates—his father and hers.

Hailey took another drink of her wine, and his damnable gaze tracked the movement of her tongue across her damp bottom lip. "Want to talk about it?" she asked.

What he wanted was to run *his* tongue along her plump bottom lip. Maybe even slip inside to taste the Prosecco lingering on her tongue and forget all about his issues with Addison.

Ahhh, clearly *that* wasn't going to happen. But as he looked across the table at Hailey, a woman who ran a successful matchmaking business and was the equivalent of a relationship guru in his eyes, it dawned on him that he had the perfect sounding board at his disposal. So why not take advantage of her expertise, especially if he ended up with a viable solution to his problem?

Decision made, he folded his arms in front of him on the table, having decided to lay out the situation for her. "Here's the deal. The texts I've been getting today are from a woman my mother set me up with, which my mom has been doing with more frequency over the past year." He tried not to grimace at how pathetic that sounded. "Anyway, Addison and I dated briefly, and after the third dinner with her, I knew that it wasn't going to work out between the two of us. So I tried to break things off, in a nice way, of course. But she's not taking the hint. Any advice?"

Mirth danced in her pretty eyes and tugged at the corner of her mouth. "Your *mother* set you up?"

Was Hailey laughing at him? Yeah, she was, not that he could blame her. What guy his age let his mother pick out his dates? Him, obviously.

"Yes, she did," he said, owning it, then explained the reason behind his mother's interference. "I'm the youngest of three siblings. And at the age of thirty, I'm also the only one who is still single. My older brother and sister are happily married with kids, and yes, my meddling mother has made it her mission to find a woman for me to settle down with so I, too, can *finally* be happy like the rest of the family." He followed that up with a sarcastic eye roll.

"I'm sure she means well," Hailey replied, propping her chin her hand, looking completely relaxed, as well as intrigued by his story. "In the matchmaking business, I come across a lot of mothers who want to find that perfect person for their son or daughter because they don't want them to end up alone."

"What my mother doesn't understand, no matter how many times I've tried to tell her, is that I'm perfectly content with my life and being a bachelor." Did he want to get married and have a family? Yes, someday, with the *right* woman. Not one his mother handpicked for him based on who she thought might make him a good wife—social status and family connections being her primary concern. And for the most part, it had been easy to deflect his mother's attempts to pair him up with someone she deemed "perfect for him," until Addison.

Their lunch order arrived, and after the waitress set a plate of gnocchi in front of him and an arugula and chicken salad for Hailey, she continued the conversation.

"If you honestly feel that way about being happy and single, then why did you agree to go out with Addison?" she asked, stabbing her fork into the leafy greens.

"Mom guilt," he said sheepishly, because it was a good portion of the truth, even if it was embarrassing. "Trust me, she's really good at getting me to do things that I'd rather not." His mother's method of persuasion was always so sweet and endearing, and he knew she meant well, which made it difficult to say no to her.

Hailey laughed, the light, amusing sound making him smile. "You're obviously a good son who loves his mom very much, and there is nothing wrong with that. It's actually a strong quality I look for when I'm interviewing my male clients. If they treat their mother with respect and hold her in high regard, that behavior usually transfers to the women he dates."

They ate a few bites of their lunches before Hailey spoke again, her expression full of genuine interest. "So, what kind of guilt tactic did your mom employ?"

This was where the story got a bit more complicated, and he tried to simplify the answer the best he could. "My father, who owns a law firm, recently had one of his biggest and wealthiest clients move from New York to Chicago. My mother became friends with the wife, and of course she met their daughter, Addison, at a few social and charity events they attended together. Then came the phone call from my mother, asking me to take Addison out for drinks or dinner because she doesn't know anyone in the city and we have *so* much in common."

"Sounds innocent enough," Hailey said, and finished off the last of her Prosecco.

"Not innocent. It was underhanded and sly," he said with a smirk as he refilled her glass, then his own. "Not in a malicious way, of course, but I know my mother. Her motivations were all about setting me up with a woman she decided was a good fit, since our families run in the same social circles. My mom honestly believed Addison was perfect for me. Those were even her exact words when she called the next day to see how our date went."

"And how *did* the date go?"

"Meh." He shrugged, the one word summing up his lack of enthusiasm for how the night had played out, and for Addison herself. "But my mother *begged* me to give Addison another chance, and yes, I succumbed to that guilt and parental pressure again," he admitted with a sigh.

Hailey's grin was priceless, as was the amusement sparkling in her eyes. His enjoyment in seeing this lighthearted side to her normally reserved personality prompted Max to continue his less-than-pleasant tale. At this point, it was more about entertaining her than anything else.

"My mom *swore* Addison had a great personality. By the end of the third date, there was no denying that my mother had lied," he said with a chuckle, trying to find humor in the situation. "That or Addison has a split personality."

Hailey gave him a sympathetic look as she set her fork on the rim of her plate, clearly done with her meal, which she'd only half eaten. "That bad, huh?"

"Addison is . . . " God, how did he politely say that she was a bitch?

"High maintenance?" Hailey suggested with a knowing glint in her gaze.

"Oh, you're good at this," he murmured, impressed with her diplomatic choice of words.

"I deal with a lot of different and extreme personalities in my business."

She shrugged her shoulders, and yeah, out of his peripheral vision, he couldn't help but notice how her full breasts bounced enticingly with the gesture. She was wearing what he guessed was a silk blouse judging by the soft-looking fabric, and while the top itself was modest, he'd already realized earlier that he could see the faint outline of her lace bra beneath.

That subtle hint of femininity was more of a turn-on to him than a woman who dressed in a way that left nothing to the imagination. Because when it came to finally getting a woman naked, removing each layer of clothing was like unwrapping a provocative present. Discovering all the arousing, delightful lingerie and bare skin and curves that lay beneath—for his eyes only—was the best part of the package.

He was pretty damn sure that beneath Hailey's prim outfits was a soft, lush body a man could lose himself in—enticing breasts made for his big hands to play with and squeeze. Tantalizing hips built for him to grab on to as he fucked her from behind. Sensual, alluring thighs designed to cushion the impact of his hard, demanding thrusts as he drove them both toward a blissful orgasm, and it was his name on her lips when she came.

"So, just how high maintenance was this woman?" Hailey asked, effectively yanking him out of his indecent thoughts with *her* in the starring role.

Finished with his lunch—of which he'd eaten every single bite—he leaned back in his chair, not in any hurry to end their time together before they went back to his office and their relationship would revert to business. "For starters, every single time Addison and I went out, she complained about *something*. The food at the restaurant not being cooked just right, no matter what it was. The wait for the valet taking too long. The wind messing up her hair that she spent two hours at the salon having styled. Half the time, I expected her to snap her fingers to make people jump to do her bidding."

A pained look of empathy passed across Hailey's features. "She sounds a little ... entitled," she said much too kindly.

"More like narcissistic," he countered more honestly, and God, it felt good to get everything off his chest since he couldn't rant to his mother about the situation. "The conversation, no matter what the topic, always ended up revolving around her, and if something happened that she didn't like, she played the victim."

He shook his head at the absurdity of it all. It didn't take him long to realize that despite how stunningly gorgeous Addison's facial features were, her beauty was all superficial. Her personality was equally artificial ... Fake laughs that grated on his nerves. Fake smiles that were condescending. Fake boobs that stood out like two firm cantaloupes on her small, too skinny frame. She walked as though she had a stick up her ass, and looked down her nose at anyone she judged as inferior. And the two times he'd kissed her, there had been no spark, no passion, and his dick hadn't so much as stirred at the possibility of getting some action. If his penis had the ability, it would have yawned from boredom.

On the other hand, Hailey was the polar opposite of Addison in every single way. The woman sitting across from him was demure and unassuming, so sweet and easy to be with and talk to, despite the fact that she was promised to another man. From the moment they'd met three months ago, she'd intrigued him. He found her fascinating and engaging and interesting, more so than any woman in a very long time.

But she is fucking engaged, you moron, so it didn't matter how attracted he was to her or how much she charmed him and his misbehaving dick, as was proven earlier today when she'd hugged him.

He shifted in his seat and finished his story. "After three dates, I couldn't take any more of Addison, and I told her at the end of the night that I wasn't feeling any chemistry, and I thought we should just be friends." He saw Hailey wince at the choice of words he'd used. "I know, I know, it's a cliché line of bullshit, right up there with the 'it's not you, it's me' sentiment, but the last thing I want is any issues between our families, considering her father is one of my father's biggest clients. I was trying to end things amicably to avoid any awkward tension between us in the future."

Their waitress came by their table to clear their plates, interrupting their conversation. They both declined dessert, and the server promised to return with the check.

Once she was gone, Hailey picked up where they'd left off. "So, how did your mom take the break-up?"

"She was definitely disappointed, but she still loves me," he said, giving her the same endearing grin that always worked to soften up his mom.

"And Addison?"

He groaned and scrubbed a hand along his jaw. "It's like we never had that last conversation. She sends me flirty texts and leaves suggestive voice messages. She's dropped by my office because she just happened to be in the area, and she has a way of showing up at events I'm attending and following me around. I stopped going to my regular coffee place in the morning because she was there every single day at the same time I got there. I even told her that I was seriously dating someone else, which only seemed to make her even more determined and persistent."

Hailey's blue eyes widened in concern. "Are you sure this isn't a *Fatal Attraction* kind of situation?"

"Trust me, it's starting to feel like it." He exhaled a harsh breath and shook his head. "But like I said, I have to be careful how I handle the situation because of the family connection, or else I probably would have done something more extreme by now."

"Like issuing a restraining order?" she suggested, her gaze glimmering with mirth.

He smirked back at her. "The thought definitely crossed my mind," he admitted.

The check arrived, and he handed over his credit card to the waitress to process the bill before glancing back at Hailey. "So, Ms. Matchmaker, how do I end this insanity with Addison?"

She braced her elbows on the table and

clasped her hands beneath her chin, the diamond on her left-hand finger annoying him with its abrasive sparkle and what it symbolized. "Well, I think you're going to have to stop avoiding and ignoring her. Agree to meet Addison somewhere, preferably a public place so she won't make a big scene. Be blunt and honest and tell her flat out that you're not interested in dating her, and the texts and the calls and the stalking need to stop," she said, then let out a small laugh. "Well, I wouldn't use the exact word *stalking*, but you get what I mean."

"I kind of like the word *stalking*," he said in a wry tone. "I certainly can't get blunter than that."

"True." She was quiet for a moment, then spoke again. "I almost don't blame Addison for stalking you. You're good-looking and successful and quite the catch. You should let me set you up. I have a ninety percent success rate when it comes to pairing up two compatible people, and I guarantee no stalkers since I do an intense and thorough pre-screening of every applicant." She grinned cheekily.

He chuckled but quickly declined her offer. "Nah, I'm more of an organic kind of guy. I prefer things to happen naturally in a relation-ship."

She looked sincerely disappointed that he'd turned her down. "Okay, but if you change your mind, you know where to find me."

"Yeah, I definitely do." He signed the receipt the server had delivered and put his credit card back into his wallet. "You ready to head over to my office and get that offer submitted?"

She nodded eagerly as she stood and settled the strap of her purse over her shoulder. "Thank you so much for lunch. It was wonder-ful."

"It was my pleasure," he said, and meant it.

He let her walk in front of him through the restaurant to the lobby, somehow managing to keep his eyes on the back of her head and not her ass. Just as they reached the entrance area, out of the corner of his eye, he saw an older woman, probably in her mid-fifties, heading toward them.

"Hailey!" the lady called out, her voice loud and enthusiastic. "I thought that was you!"

Hailey's entire body stiffened, and reluctant-ly, she turned toward the other woman, who was now standing in front of her. A smile that seemed forced tipped up the corners of her mouth as she exchanged air kisses with the stylishly dressed woman who reminded him of his own mother.

"Maureen!" Hailey said once they were done with their faux kisses, her voice pitched higher than normal as she deliberately eased in front of Max. "It's so good to see you. How are Brian and Tiffany?"

Maureen grabbed Hailey's hand in hers and gave it a gentle pat. "They are doing well. *Very* well," she said cheerfully. "Dare I say I see an engagement in their future? You couldn't have matched them any more perfectly than you did. They are like two peas in a pod, and absolutely adorable together. I don't think I've ever seen my son so happy."

"I'm glad to hear it," Hailey replied, that slight tension still straining her voice. "They were one of my favorite couples to match," she said, which told Max that she'd obviously found this woman's son the new love of his life.

Maureen openly glanced around Hailey, a curious gleam in her eyes as she gave Max an appreciative once-over. He smiled at her in return, waiting for some kind of cue or signal from Hailey . . . which never came. It was as though she was pretending that he didn't exist.

"So, who is this nice-looking gentleman that you're with?" Maureen prompted unabashedly.

Max stepped next to Hailey's side again and glanced at her face, fully expecting an introduction. Hailey's lips parted slightly, but no words came out, and unmistakable dread etched her features.

What the hell was going on? Everything about this situation was so out of character for Hailey, and her behavior didn't make any sense at all.

Finally, words starting coming out of Hailey's mouth. "This is ummm... ahhh..." she stammered anxiously, her eyes wild with panic. "He's...ummm."

What. The. Fuck? He stared at Hailey incredulously, and since she seemed oddly flustered and incapable of stringing a sentence together, Max extended his hand toward Maureen and took over the introductions for her. "I'm Max Sterling, Hailey's—"

"Oh, my God!" Maureen gasped dramatically, not giving him the chance to finish what he'd been about to say, that he was Hailey's real estate broker. "Finally, I get to meet your elusive and very handsome fiancé!"

Fiancé? Wait... *what?*

His mind put on some major mental brakes. He wasn't sure how Maureen had come to *that* mistaken conclusion, and he glanced at Hailey, fully expecting her to jump in and correct the other woman's assumption.

Instead, those big blue eyes of hers were desperately pleading with him to *please* play along with the charade, and even though he was perplexed and conflicted—because *what the fuck?*—it was that imploring look, those distressed features, that influenced him to impersonate her fiancé.

Or did she even *have* a fiancé? Because if she did, wouldn't she just admit that Max wasn't him? Jesus, he was so damned confused.

Deciding he'd get answers once they were alone again, Max followed through on Hailey's silent pleading look and posed as the man she was engaged to, as strange as that was. She wanted him to pretend they were in love, that he was the man who adored her? Challenge accepted.

Buckle up and get ready for a wild ride, baby.

Picking up Hailey's left hand, he tucked it into the crook of his arm, effectively pulling her closer to his side. Her engagement ring winked up at him, and he suddenly hated that it belonged to another man.

Or did it?

Playing his part, he inclined his head at the other woman, who was staring at him as though he was some kind of prince charming, and gave her a charismatic smile. "It's an absolute pleasure to meet you, Maureen."

Hailey's body visibly relaxed, her relief palpable that he'd cooperated.

Maureen sighed wistfully, her gaze softening as she took them in as a couple. "Just look at the two of you. You look so in love." She pressed a hand to her heart. "I don't think I've ever seen such a pretty flush on Hailey's face. You must be doing a very good job of keeping her happy." She winked at him.

Max chuckled, liking Maureen despite the bizarre situation he'd found himself in, and he was certain that Hailey's pink cheeks were due to panic, not adoration.

"I try my best. I know she certainly keeps *me* happy." He lifted the back of Hailey's hand to his lips and placed a lingering kiss on her knuckles. Desire thrummed through his veins when he heard her soft inhale of breath that told him how much his touch affected her. "Yes, I'm a very lucky man."

"Yes, you are, and don't you forget it." Maureen waggled a finger at him, just like his mother would. "Hailey is a keeper."

"I knew that the moment I saw her," he said, pouring it on thick. "Now that I have a ring on her finger, she's all mine."

"You're also a very smart man." Maureen's smile never wavered. "I'm so glad to finally meet you. You've turned down so many invitations to dinners and events the past three months, I was beginning to think that you didn't really exist."

Now that was an interesting tidbit. And more pieces fell into place. As soon as Max had introduced himself using his name, the woman had realized he was Hailey's fiancé. Hailey had a fiancé *named Max Sterling* who never attended events with his girlfriend. Jesus. Had Hailey created a fake fiancé based on him?

With that crazy possibility rolling around in his head, he grinned at Maureen. "Well, now you have proof that I'm not a figment of Hailey's imagination," he teased with a wink at the other woman.

"He's just a very busy man," Hailey jumped in quickly. "Just like I told you."

"Yes, you did," Maureen replied with a nod

before meeting Max's gaze again. "You're in the real estate business, right?"

Hailey had even used his occupation? He was beginning to feel like he was being punked or was in the Twilight Zone. "Yes, that's correct," he confirmed, because it was certainly the truth.

Maureen sighed, her expression turning to disappointment. "It's really such a shame you can't make it to the charity event at the end of the month with Hailey."

Max felt his new fiancée tense against his side, and when he glanced at her, her eyes spoke volumes. *Please, just go with it and express your regrets.* Oh, he was definitely going to *go with it,* but not in the way she was hoping or expected.

Instead of agreeing with Maureen and making an excuse for his absence, he frowned at Hailey. "Sweetheart, I don't remember you mentioning a charity event to me."

She looked taken aback for a moment, clearly not expecting him to make an issue out of the situation. Then, she gave him a tight smile. "You had a prior commitment, *remember?*"

"It's such a shame, too," Maureen said, oblivious to the silent battle going on between him and Hailey. "The charity carnival is for Mercy Home for Boys & Girls, and it would have been great to have an extra pair of hands for the setup and heavy lifting. We can use all the extra help we can get."

"I know. I'm very disappointed that he won't be there, too," Hailey said quickly. "But I understand how important Max's work is to him."

"Not as important as *you are* to me," he replied, trying not to laugh at the frustration Hailey was conveying with her pretty blue eyes. "I didn't realize how much this charity event meant to you. What weekend is it again?"

Hailey's jaw clenched stubbornly, even as a sweet smile managed to play across her lips for their audience's sake. "I can't remember off-hand."

Max shifted his gaze back to Maureen, and the other woman immediately and helpfully shared the date of the event since Hailey was having a temporary mental lapse. He pretended to think it over, but he already knew he had nothing scheduled that on that particular weekend. He was *all* hers, whether she wanted him or not.

"You know what? That prior commitment really isn't that important," he said, being a good fiancé and making it all about Hailey and not himself. "I can switch things around so I can have the entire weekend free."

Hailey's fingers clutched at his arm. "Max, you don't need to do that." Her voice was indulgent, even though he was intensely aware of the warning in her grip.

He refused to let her off the hook. She'd dragged him into this fake engagement, and now she was about to bear the consequences of her actions. Turning toward her, he lifted his hands and framed her face in his palms, the gesture so intimate that Hailey's eyes widened with shock at his bold move. He merely smiled and gave her an adoring look to match his next words.

"Sweetheart, I know I don't *need* to do it," he drawled in a husky tone. "I *want* to do it."

"Oh, my. I guess that settles that," Maureen said with a pleased laugh. "I'll be seeing you *both* at the charity event."

Max let Hailey witness the satisfaction he knew was reflecting in his gaze before he released his hold on her and glanced back at the other woman. "Yes, you absolutely will," he promised her.

"Wonderful." Maureen beamed at both of them. "I've taken up enough of your time and should let the two of you go, and I need to get back to my lunch date. Hailey, so lovely seeing you, and Max, it's been a pleasure to finally meet you after all this time."

Max shook the woman's hand once more and bestowed a dazzling smile her way. "The pleasure is all mine."

They said their good-byes, and as Max watched Maureen walk away, his mind reeled with a million different questions for Hailey, and he didn't even know where to start. Was she really engaged? Did she even have a fiancé? And why had she used *his* name and occupation as part of the pretense? He was baffled, intrigued, and a part of him also felt duped. As much as he wanted to demand answers to all his questions, Spiaggia wasn't the place to confront her.

Grabbing Hailey's hand tight in his to make sure she didn't try and bolt on him, he pulled her toward the restaurant's front door. Just as he suspected, she tried to tug her hand from his grasp, but he wasn't letting her go. Not until they settled a few things.

"Max," she said, her desperate voice hitting him just as they stepped out onto the busy sidewalk. "Let me explain. Please."

Oh, he intended to let her explain everything, but at the moment, there was so much for him to process, and he needed time to calm the fuck down so they could have a rational conversation when his head wasn't spinning. So, he said nothing as he led her toward his office building, his quick strides forcing her to trot beside him in her heels to keep up with his pace.

"Max," she tried again, her voice breathless from their brisk walk. "I know this looks really bad, and I'm sorry that—"

He stopped abruptly in front of his office building, so fast he cut off her words and she nearly collided into him. "Don't say another word," he said gruffly. She'd just put him through the wringer, and what happened from here forward was going to be on *his* terms.

Genuine contrition darkened her blue eyes. "But—"

"Not. Another. Fucking. Word."

She bit her bottom lip and stared up at him anxiously, but clearly realizing just how on edge he was, she obeyed his order and kept quiet.

With her hand still tight in his, he continued into the building and onto the first elevator that arrived on the lobby floor. The doors slid closed with just the two of them inside. Standing so close to Hailey in a confined space, he could hear her breathing, the sensual sound heightening the awareness between them now that they were completely alone. That soft, floral scent of hers surrounded him, teasing his senses and triggering that desire he'd harbored for Hailey for too damn long.

For three long fucking months, he'd wanted Hailey, and he'd spent all that time believing his attraction to her was forbidden and she was off-limits. But even knowing that, it hadn't stopped him from fantasizing about her or imagining the feel of her body beneath his and wondering what her soft moans of pleasure might sound like when she climaxed. Late at night, alone in his own bed with his hand clasped firmly around his shaft, he'd envisioned *her* soft lips wrapped around his cock and the needy look in her eyes as she looked up at him and sucked him off.

His jaw clenched tight as the elevator ascended the floors. For three long fucking months, he'd *hated* that he was the asshole who secretly lusted after a woman who wore another man's ring on her finger. Publicly, he'd never made a move on her, never given her any indication that he was attracted to her or acted inappropriate in any way. As difficult as it had been for him, he'd respected what that ring had represented.

Had his gentlemanly behavior all been in vain? That was the million-dollar question nagging at him.

Before they went any further, in this elevator and between them, there was one thing he absolutely needed to know. Reaching out, he pressed the red STOP button, bringing the lift to a halt between floors. He turned around and closed the two short steps separating them, until she was backed up against the wall and he had his hands braced on either side of her shoulders—not that there was anywhere for her to escape to.

"Max?" she asked softly.

He heard the uncertainty in her voice, but she didn't look afraid or intimidated, which wasn't his intent anyway. He watched her tongue slick across her bottom lip nervously, and a sharp jolt of arousal punched him in the gut. Keeping a tight rein on his control until he had the answer he sought, he lifted his gaze back up to her wide-eyed one.

"Just tell me one thing right now," he said,

his voice a bit raspy and his pulse racing. "You've worn an engagement ring the entire time I've known you, leading me to believe you were taken. After what just happened back at the restaurant, you owe me an honest answer to the question I'm about to ask you."

"Okay," she whispered.

"Do you have a fiancé? A boyfriend? *Any* man in your life right now?"

She shook her head. "No. No one."

"Thank fucking God," he muttered and did what he'd been dying to do for three goddamn months. He pushed his hands into her hair, tipped her head back, and crushed his mouth to hers.

Chapter Three

AS SOON AS Max's lips pressed against Hailey's, she gasped in shock, completely taken aback by the impulsive move she hadn't seen coming, as well as the unapologetic demand of his mouth claiming hers. From the start, there was nothing gentle about the kiss. Nothing remotely tentative about the way his tongue boldly pushed past her parted lips, swept deep inside, and tangled sensuously with hers.

She moaned softly, breathlessly, as a surge of arousal spilled through her veins, causing her stomach to quiver and her legs to tremble. When it came to men and kissing them, nothing in Hailey's past experiences had prepared her for *this* man's hot, hungry, and immediate assault on her senses. She was used to nice, pleasant, uninspiring kisses, due to her habit of deliberately ending things with her dates before anything more passionate could develop.

In one fell swoop, Max had bypassed polite and respectful and dived straight into greedy and ravenous. The man who'd been the epitome of an honorable gentleman the past three months was no longer courteous and well-mannered, as he effortlessly stripped away her ability to resist him with a bold kiss that made her melt deep inside.

Another stroke of his tongue, and she tasted the heat of his desire. And when he pressed his lower body directly against hers, she felt the hard length of his erection straining the front of his trousers, which ignited a slow burn of need between her legs. Her breasts swelled and her nipples tightened, chafing against the lace lining in her bra.

Seemingly of their own accord, her curious hands slid beneath his suit jacket, her fingers encountering the firm muscle of his abdomen beneath his dress shirt. He groaned in the back of his throat and deepened the kiss even more. Before she lost the nerve, or Max realized just how inept she was when it came to *any* of this, she skimmed her palms up to his chest, then around to his back and down the muscled slope of his spine.

God, he was gorgeous and sexier than sin. Everything about him was so hard and solid and perfectly sculpted, making her suddenly acutely aware of how soft and curvy and flawed she was in comparison, when he was probably used to svelte, sophisticated women who knew how to satisfy an experienced man like him. And before she could stop them, her insecurities wormed their way into her head and tainted her thoughts, effectively ruining the most pleasurable, sensual moment of her life.

Before she could end the kiss, Max lifted his mouth from hers, his warm breath caressing her damp lips and his eyes dark and hot as they stared into hers. He was breathing as hard as she was, but he didn't move away. The hands twisted in her hair moved down to her jaw, and the soft, tender stroke of his thumb along her cheek belied his tense expression as he studied her face much too intently.

"We're not done with this conversation," he said in a deep, rough voice that was just as assertive as his uncompromising stance in front of her. "We have business to take care of and an offer to submit once we get to the office, and then you're going to tell me how I became your fiancé without me even knowing it. Understand?"

She swallowed hard and nodded her head, even though she knew he wasn't really giving her an option on the matter. "Yes." At the very least, she owed him the truth, no matter how awkward it might be.

Satisfied with her answer, he stepped away and released the stop button. The elevator continued its upward climb, and beside her, Max exhaled a deep breath and dragged his hands through his hair, as if trying to collect his composure. She couldn't read his mood, but she could easily assume that he was less than pleased with her at the moment, not that she could blame him.

The doors to the elevator opened, and without a word, she walked out first, a little surprised, and unnerved, by the subtle press of his hand at the base of her spine. The touch felt . . . possessive, and definitely intimate, and she wasn't sure what to make of the gesture. Especially considering what had just transpired between them, and she wasn't referring to that angry kiss, but her deception.

She'd been to Max's office many times over

the past three months, and she knew the way to his reception area, where his pretty and young secretary, Olivia, was sitting behind a desk, typing away on her computer keyboard.

She glanced up and smiled when she saw them approaching. "Good afternoon, Hailey," she said cheerfully, then looked at Max. "The purchase agreement for the property in Logan Square is on your desk for you to look over."

"Thank you, Olivia," he replied with a curt nod. "Will you please take Hailey to the conference room?"

"Sure." Olivia came around her desk, a slight frown creasing her brow as she watched Max walk down the hallway toward his office. "What's up with him?" she murmured, more to herself than anyone else.

Clearly, Olivia wasn't used to her boss being so terse. Truth be told, Hailey had never seen Max this way, either—he was always so easy-going and good-natured—and even though she knew she was to blame for his brusque attitude, she wasn't about to tell his secretary the *reason* and drag her into their current drama.

Olivia led the way to the conference room. "Would you like something to drink?" she asked once they arrived.

She wondered, just briefly, if she ought to ask for a shot of something strong and alcoholic but decided she needed to be clear-headed for this meeting . . . and the confrontation ahead.

"A glass of water would be wonderful, thank you." Hailey took a corner seat at the long mahogany table while Olivia set a cold bottle of water and a glass in front of her, then the younger woman excused herself and headed back to her desk.

Hailey rubbed her fingers across her forehead, then poured herself a glass of water and took a much-needed swallow of the cool liquid. Now that she was alone, a nervous energy swirled inside of her because she knew she had to fess up all the embarrassing details of her deception to Max. And with it so quiet in the room, it gave her mind too much time to replay the encounter with Maureen, and Max's response to it all.

She was grateful that he'd gone along with the ruse without calling her out in front of Maureen—because he easily could have, and that would have really shot her credibility as a reputable matchmaker all to hell. Instead, he'd played the part of her loving fiancé—almost too well, she thought with a grimace. The man could certainly act, because his performance had been Oscar worthy and Maureen had fallen for Max's charming personality and displays of affection.

He'd gone above and beyond, but it was the change in him once they were outside the restaurant and alone again that she found perplexing. He'd gone from effortlessly winning Maureen over with his wit and sparkling conversation to cool and uptight on the power walk to his office building. But it was that hot, deep, spontaneous kiss in the elevator that still had her head spinning, because all that sexual tension he'd unleashed on her had seemingly come out of nowhere.

Or had it?

Confusion swirled through her, and she touched her fingers to her lips, still swollen from the deliciously aggressive treatment of Max's mouth on hers. In three months' time, he'd never given her any indication that he was attracted to her, but that kiss . . . well, it had bypassed basic attraction and had been filled with unmistakable lust.

It was far easier for Hailey to believe that he'd kissed her out of anger or punishment. And truthfully, his behavior in the elevator might have been a result of his frustration with her, but there was no doubt in her mind that it hadn't *ended* that way. By the time he'd withdrawn his lips from hers and she looked into his intoxicating gaze, the undeniable heat she saw there was laced with one hundred percent desire. *For her.*

A shiver stole through her at that realization, and she pressed her thighs together to ease the persistent ache he'd started with that kiss.

"Looks like everything on the purchase agreement is just as we discussed," Max said from behind her as he entered the room, carrying a sheath of papers.

Hailey had been so caught up in her thoughts that she didn't hear him arrive and jumped in her seat when he spoke. He sat down at the end of the table, which put him diagonally next to her chair, and spread the papers out in front of him. She noticed that he'd taken off his suit jacket and had rolled up the sleeves of his shirt to reveal his strong forearms, which only made him look sexier.

Other than his ruffled hair, he was a man in total control. Everything about him was all business, as if that kiss between them had never happened. His expression was devoid of any tangible emotion, and she realized that she wanted the old Max back. The one who was quick to smile and made her laugh. The one she felt comfortable around and at ease with. The one she'd come to think of as a friend.

Had she completely screwed up everything by making him a part of her fake engagement? Her stomach hurt with the possibility.

"We'll go over all the terms before you sign the agreement," he went on in a straightforward manner. "And then we'll send it over to Daniel, the current owner of the property, for his approval and signature, as well. Once that's done, we'll start the title search, order an appraisal, and set up a property inspection."

She nodded. "Okay."

Hailey knew this was going to be a fairly fast process, especially with the owner asking for a quick turnaround on the sale of the property, which was what she also wanted. Her fifty percent cash down payment had already been verified, and she was pre-approved for financing. A thirty-day escrow was doable.

Over the next half hour, Max explained all the pertinent details of the purchase and sale agreement in a professional and efficient manner. He was patient with her questions and treated the entire transaction like the business deal it was. Once she approved all the terms and signed the contract, Max pressed the button on the intercom on the table. A few seconds later, his secretary answered and he requested her presence in the conference room.

She arrived, and Max handed her the documents. "I need you to email this offer to Daniel Morrison for his approval and signature, which he's expecting. Let me know as soon as he returns the agreement and if he's requested any changes, or if he accepts the terms as stated so we can get this property into escrow as quickly as possible."

"Sure thing," Olivia said, and turned to go.

"And please shut the door when you leave," he added, his dark greenish-brown eyes focused directly on Hailey.

Olivia did as he asked, and as soon as the two of them were alone in the silent room, Max leaned back in his leather chair, looking very much in charge and emanating a confidence that made her pulse escalate a few beats. While she'd always enjoyed his lighthearted side, this controlled version made her very aware of him as a man, and mostly on a sexual level. And now, after that kiss and having intimate knowledge of how it felt to have his strong, hard frame pressed up against hers, her sorely deprived body wanted more.

Max tipped his head, regarding her in a way she couldn't define. "Now that the most important thing is taken care of and out of the way, and I've had the chance to really think about what happened at the restaurant, you and I have a few things to discuss."

She didn't miss the small smirk on his lips that told her he liked having the upper hand, and she clasped her hands in her lap to keep her fingers from fidgeting. *Let the mortification begin.* "What would you like to know?"

"We've already established that there is currently no man in your life, fiancé or otherwise," he said, dropping his gaze to the mouth he'd ravished a short while ago before slowly raising his eyes back to hers. "So why are you wearing a ring on your finger that leads people to believe you're engaged?"

There was no judgment or criticism in his tone, which chased away some of her anxiety, but certainly not all of it because she still had to explain her reasons for doing something so extreme. Not an easy feat when her logic for creating a fake fiancé was humiliating to admit.

Then again, she'd never believed she'd ever be in the position to have to confess the pretense of being engaged to anyone.

"I'm a reputable, high-profile matchmaker, and my own track record with men kind of sucks, which completely contradicts what I do for a living," she said, pushing out the shameful truth. Or most of it, anyway. There were some things that didn't need to be a part of this conversation—like the fact that *she* was the one responsible for every one of those failed relationships.

"After my last break-up about six months ago, I decided to take a sabbatical from dating and focus on building the Ellison Agency instead," she continued, absently tapping the toe of one of her shoes on the floor. "I didn't want any distractions, and it was just easier to put a ring on my finger and to perpetuate the lie of being engaged and to ward off any interest my clients might have in me, which has happened a few times."

"Well, the ring certainly fooled me," he said, his features softening a bit.

She was happy to see the old Max resurfacing, and was grateful that he didn't ask about her inability to sustain a relationship with a guy.

The answer to that was far more complicated and wasn't something she wanted to discuss with Max. It was hard enough that she was self-conscious about her body image, even after losing so much weight, and her insecurities weren't relevant to this conversation, anyway.

He drummed his fingers on the leather armrest of his chair, his body seemingly more relaxed, as if he'd found her reasons for the pretense somewhat justifiable. "So, I guess we're at the part where you tell me how my name got pulled into your little charade."

Before she even said a word, a warm flush crept up her neck and swept across her cheeks. Feeling restless, she pushed herself out of her chair and walked over to the windows in the conference room that overlooked the city of Chicago. God, this part of the story was, well, *awkward*, to say the least. But again, she owed Max an explanation, and after crossing her arms over her chest, she turned around and forced herself to give him the answers he deserved to hear.

"For the first few months of wearing the engagement ring, none of my clients questioned it or asked about my significant other." Some of them had offered congratulations, but surprisingly no one asked for a name, which had made it easy for her to get complacent about the fiancé fabrication.

"What about family and friends?" he questioned curiously as he swiveled his chair to face her, presenting her with a full-length view of his big body sprawled so casually before her. "What do they believe?"

"My family doesn't live in Chicago," she told him, forgoing the fact that her parents were dead and her aunt and uncle had been the ones to raise her. Another story for another time, if ever. "They live in Springfield, so I only see them once or twice a year, so it's not an issue. My best friend and assistant at the agency, Brielle, is the only one who knows the truth."

He nodded, and she finished answering his initial question. "Anyway, it was shortly after you and I met three months ago when I ran into Maureen, who has a lot of connections and has referred quite a few clients to me since her son started dating Tiffany. The first thing she noticed was the ring on my finger, and she demanded to know who the man in my life was. I tried to be evasive, but you saw for yourself how persistent she can be."

He chuckled, the sound deep and amused,

just how she liked it best. "Yeah, just a little bit."

She breathed a sigh of relief, that he was coming around and she was seeing glimpses of the Max she knew and loved . . . crap, not loved as in *love*, she quickly amended for the second time that day. But she'd definitely grown very fond of him and his swoon-worthy traits and quirks over the past three months. After the kiss in the elevator, she'd feared that it would be a while before she saw that engaging man again, and she was thankful that he'd returned so quickly.

"It was that day you took me to see that building in Avondale," she reminded him, back to twisting the engagement ring around her finger again. "I'd just left your office, so you were on my mind and I just blurted out your name . . . " Her eyes immediately widened. *Oh, shit.* Too late, she realized just how much she'd revealed in that one little sentence.

Max arched a brow as he slowly stood and strolled over to where she was standing. "Am I on your mind a lot, Hailey?" he asked in a low, husky murmur.

His voice made her insides quiver and caused her nipples to tighten into hard points.

Now that he knew there wasn't a fiancé, he didn't even try to disguise the fact that he noticed her body's reaction, and he liked what he saw.

"I'm not sure what you mean?" she said, trying to keep her own voice steady.

The beginnings of a wicked smile curved his lips, and he lifted his hand and wound a strand of her long, blonde hair around his finger, ensnaring her in more ways than one. "I'm sure you know *exactly* what I mean," he countered, his gaze holding hers hostage. "I've spent the past three months thinking about you, more than I should have, considering I believed you were engaged. Want to know what I fantasized about?"

Her lips parted, but she was suddenly unable to speak. Her mind knew she ought to tell him *no*, but when his free hand settled on the curve of her waist and he stepped closer, the only thing that managed to escape her throat was a soft, needy moan of acquiescence.

Satisfaction gleamed in his eyes. "I'll take that as a yes." His head moved to the side of hers so that his lips were at her ear. "I thought constantly about kissing you, and now that that I know how sweet you taste, I want so much more. I've wondered what your naked breasts look like, how your nipples would respond when I scrape my thumbnails across those hard points."

"*Max*," she breathed heavily, both shocked and thrilled by his explicit descriptions.

The hand at her waist skimmed along her hip and around to her backside in a seductive caress that left tingles of warmth in its wake. Completely aroused, she wavered on her feet and stumbled back a step, only to have the window ledge behind her bring her up short. Which gave Max the perfect opportunity to crowd in closer.

She realized he was playing by his own rules now, and she was suddenly on the losing end of the game. She wasn't used to a man's single-minded determination to seduce her, and it was hard for her to believe that it was gorgeous, sexy Max who was touching her so provocatively and tempting her with his dirty talk. How was she supposed to resist his brand of persuasion?

"This is one big mess and I'm so sorry," she said, desperately trying to keep him at bay. "I . . . I never thought it would come to this." She wasn't sure if she meant the truth being exposed about her using Max as her fake fiancé or this attraction between them that was making her so weak with wanting him. No, she hadn't seen that one coming at all, and his interest in her that way threw her completely off-kilter.

"Ahhh, but it *did* come to this," he refuted, his full, generous mouth easing into a too inviting smile. "The big question is, what are we going to do about it?"

Chapter Four

MAX KNEW HE had Hailey cornered, literally and figuratively. He had his body situated in front of hers and the hand he had firmly on her ass kept her from breaking free like he sensed she was on the verge of doing, and he knew her flight instincts weren't because she didn't want him. No, there was no doubt in his mind that his attraction to her was fully reciprocated. A woman didn't let a man kiss her the deep, thorough way he had in the elevator without some basis of desire driving her response.

Yet there was something about the undeniable chemistry between them that was making her anxious. He could feel it in her tense body language when he touched her, could sense it in the sensual push-pull between them. And he could definitely see it in her wide blue eyes as they stared up at him right this moment, filled with a wealth of doubts.

It was as if she found it difficult to believe he could want her. She'd mentioned that her track record with men wasn't great, and he was suddenly curious to know more but was smart enough to realize that asking such a personal question would probably do more harm than good right now.

So, instead, he focused on their current predicament and where they were going from here now that the cat was out of the bag, so to speak. He took a step away from her, sliding his hand from her backside and releasing the silky hair still entwined around his finger.

She exhaled a deep breath, looking relieved . . . and disappointed that he'd moved away. "You don't have to go to the charity event, Max," Hailey said on a rush, clearly attempting to cut any ties to him beyond business. "I'll come up with some kind of believable excuse to appease Maureen."

He tipped his head and pushed his hands into the front pockets of his trousers. Did she really think he was going to let her off so easily?

Apparently so. However, he'd already decided that if posing as her fake fiancé was the only way to see if whatever was between them could develop into something more, then he had no qualms using the pretense as an excuse. Besides, he realized that this whole fabricated engagement scenario could work to his advantage, as well.

"I'm not about to let you disappoint Maureen," he said, resting his backside against the edge of the conference table behind him. "And since you conjured up our fake relationship, and I'm going to help keep your reputation as a matchmaker intact, I think you owe me something in return."

She blinked at him, that wariness returning. "And what would that be?"

"This fake engagement of ours is going to help me get rid of Addison and make my mother stop with her awful matchmaking attempts. She doesn't pre-screen like you do, which is how I ended up with a stalker," he said with a humorous grin, and was gratified to see her mouth tip up in a smile, too. "My mother is throwing a big party for my father's sixtieth birthday. It's a casual outdoor barbeque, and Addison and her parents will be there as well, so it's the perfect opportunity to introduce you to everyone as my fiancée."

She chewed on her thumbnail for a few moments as she considered his request, her expression skeptical. "Your family would believe that you got engaged to a woman so quickly?"

"They should." He shrugged and braced his hands on the edge of the table. "My grandparents got married six weeks after they met, and my parents eloped three months after their first date, so quick engagements run in the family."

Her brows rose in surprise. "Wow. Okay," she said, his explanation convincing her. "But at some point, we're going to have to figure out a way to end our engagement. I mean, this can't go on forever."

He laughed, and she grinned impishly. "Did you not think about that when you initially came up with this whole fake fiancé idea?"

"Honestly, no."

She winced and blushed at that confession, and all Max could think was that she was fucking adorable, and he had to resist the urge to pull her into his arms and kiss her again—but this time slower, softer. She was so candid and guileless, and so completely opposite of any woman he'd ever dated, which was a huge part of her appeal to him.

She sighed as she glanced at the diamond on her finger. "I just thought when I was ready to take the ring off, which probably wasn't going to be for a long while, I was going to say we split amicably."

"How about you not worry about all that for now?" He was more than willing to see where this pretend relationship took them, and this would give him the chance to really get to know her and vice versa. "When the time comes, we'll stage some kind of believable break-up."

But even as he said the words, which were meant to reassure her, the thought of never seeing her again made his gut twist with opposition and made him wonder just how much he'd fallen for Hailey in the past three months that he'd known her, despite believing she was engaged.

More than he realized, he thought, startled by the revelation. He wasn't in love with her, but now that he knew she was free and clear and available, he definitely *felt* something for her.

She was standing close enough that he was able to reach out, gently grasp her wrist, and pull her toward him. Surprisingly, she didn't resist or panic at his open display of affection—which he figured she needed to get used to, anyway—and he moved his feet apart, making room for her in between his legs. They were now face-to-face and only inches apart, her lush mouth tempting him.

"*Max . . .*" she said when he settled his hands on her waist, those uncertainties infusing her voice again.

"Hailey . . . " he teased right back, and was gratified when the beginnings of a smile appeared on her lips. "You're going to have to learn to relax around me. Especially when I'm touching you."

A small frown furrowed her brows as she tipped her head forward, causing that thick, gorgeous hair of hers to fall in soft waves down to her breasts. "I'm just not used to a guy being so . . ."

"Handsy?" he supplied for her, and deliberately skimmed his palms lower, drifting them down her hips to where her thighs began, just to accentuate his point.

She shifted on her heels, seemingly self-conscious with the intimate way he was touching her, even through her clothing. "Well, that's one way of putting it."

He wasn't sure what to make of her unease, but he wasn't about to let her be insecure with him. "Get used to it, sweetheart." Because if he had his way, his hands were going to be all over her beautiful, curvy body. "In fact, there's one more important thing about this arrangement of ours. Since I'm agreeing to be your fake fiancé, then I'm going to have to insist that I get all the benefits that go with it."

He heard her quick intake of breath, saw the hesitation flickering in her eyes as her gaze searched his face. "Are you saying you want to sleep with me?"

Abso-fucking-lutely. Yeah, he didn't think that particular answer would go over too well at the moment, so he tempered his response and added a grin. "For the sake of full disclosure, I certainly wouldn't say no if the offer was on the table."

She rolled her eyes, looking adorable again. "Well, for the sake of full disclosure, it probably won't happen."

He chuckled, and actually liked the fact that she was discriminating when it came to sex. Another refreshing thing about her, compared to many of the other women he'd dated, who'd made it clear they were willing to put out on the first night. But there was a *probably* in her statement, which meant she wasn't flat out rejecting the *possibility* of it happening. They'd just have to wait and see where things between them led and go from there.

"So, about those benefits," he said, bringing them back to his stipulations. "During the course of our engagement, for however long it lasts, I want the freedom to touch you and kiss you anytime I want."

She pursed her lips as she debated his request, which didn't help her cause since it only emphasized how sensual her mouth was.

He wasn't asking for anything that they hadn't already done, and decided he needed to be a bit more persuasive. He brought his hands up to her face, holding her far more gently than he had in the elevator as he drew her mouth closer and closer to his. She didn't resist him or try to pull back, but neither did she surrender, and that's what he wanted the most. Her sweet capitulation.

"Come on, sweet girl," he cajoled, her lips less than an inch away from his. "You know you want me to kiss you again. All you have to do is say yes to the kissing and touching . . . "

On an unraveling moan, her lashes fluttered closed, her body relaxed, and she breathed the one word he was desperate to hear. "Yes."

Satisfaction surged through him, and he finally brought her mouth to his, meshing their lips in slow, measured degrees until they were completely fused. Unlike the wild kiss in the elevator, this time he lingered and explored, learning the shape of her mouth against his and savoring the feel and taste of her. He sucked and nibbled at her lower lip, enjoying the husky moan of pleasure that escaped her, and reveled in the way her body swayed closer to his of its own accord.

His dick responded to that small victory as he tipped her head slightly, then gradually, languidly took the kiss deeper. He slid his tongue inside, teasing and flirting with hers. The give and take was playful and sexy, without demands or expectations, and by the time he eased back and ended the kiss, Hailey was smiling, her stunning blue eyes hazy with desire.

He smiled, too. "Just so you know, there's going to be a lot of kissing and touching. Anything beyond that, we can negotiate," he said with a devilish wink.

✧　✧　✧

"OH. MY. GOD."

Hailey bit back a grin at Brielle's response to the entire story she'd just relayed to her best friend about her whirlwind day with Max and everything that had happened between them—from the encounter with Maureen at the restaurant to the mind-blowing kiss in the elevator to Max eventually agreeing to be her fake fiancé.

And right after that second kiss with Max, and his teasing remark about negotiating anything more, the owner for the property in Logan Square had called to tell Max that he'd accepted the offer for the building, and the signed paperwork was on its way over. Hailey had been bouncing by the time she returned to her own office, nearly bursting with excitement to share the news with her best friend, who'd insisted they head out to one of the hot spots in Chicago, the Popped Cherry, for a celebratory drink after work.

After sliding into a vacant booth and ordering a cosmopolitan and an appetizer of stuffed mushrooms for the two of them to share, Hailey spent the next half an hour spilling *all* the details of her afternoon with Max. Brielle was the one and only person in her life that she shared everything with. They'd been best friends since her freshman year at University of Chicago, when they were paired up to share a room together in the campus dorms. After graduation, it had been Brielle who'd encouraged Hailey to start her matchmaking business because, believe it or not, she had a knack for setting up compatible couples and had been doing it since high school with her friends.

The woman sitting across from Hailey knew her deepest secrets, fears, and insecurities—and loved her anyway. Besides being her assistant at the Ellison Agency and overall marketing expert, and despite the two of them being on opposite ends of the personality spectrum—Brielle was more bubbly and outgoing to Hailey's more quiet and introspective nature—she was the sister Hailey had never had, and she didn't know what she would do without Brielle in her life.

"The whole thing with Max is crazy, right?" Hailey finally said with a shake of her head, once she'd brought her friend up to speed on the arrangement she and Max had agreed to.

Brielle finished the last stuffed mushroom on the table between them and sat back in her seat with a huge grin on her face as she summed up their conversation. "Let's see . . . between those sizzling-hot kisses and making your pretend engagement to one of the sexiest men in Chicago official and purchasing the building of your dreams, I'd say you've had the best day *ever*."

Hailey laughed and couldn't disagree. She was still on a high about her new digs, and still a little buzzed from having Max's mouth on hers. Twice. Even though both times had been so different in intensity, there was no denying that the man knew how to kiss . . . and if she wasn't such a prim and proper good girl with more than a few hang-ups, her very damp panties probably would have dropped to the floor both times.

She crossed her legs beneath the table to subdue the ache that still lingered and gave Brielle the one last piece of information she'd withheld until now. "He said he's willing to negotiate more than just kissing and touching during our temporary agreement."

Brielle's brown eyes lit up with renewed interest. "And that's a problem because . . .?"

Hailey frowned at Brielle's enthusiasm on her behalf and threw a crumpled napkin at her. "You *know* why, smartass." It had been a long time since they'd had this specific conversation, but she knew what her best friend was insinuating and where this discussion would most likely lead.

"Yes, I know *exactly* why." Brielle sighed, her expression turning serious. "I just think it's past time that you put yourself out there that way again."

Hailey finished the last of her cosmopolitan and arched a brow. "That way?"

"Sex," Brielle said succinctly, the one word that always made Hailey cringe when it pertained to her specifically. "You've been with one asshole, and that was back in college. He fucked you once, and he wasn't even polite enough to give you an orgasm for taking your virginity, and then the dickwad douchebag had the nerve to send you a demeaning, obnoxious break-up text the next day. And every guy you've dated since then, *you've* ended things before you get to the main event. It's past time to get your groove back on, sister."

Hailey knew she was a self-sabotager when it came to her relationships. But in all honesty, out of all the guys she'd dated who'd matched well with her on paper and when it came to a compatibility quiz, none had ever made her *want* to take that next intimate step with them where she bared her entire body—the soft belly, the stretch marks from the weight loss, the less-than-firm backside.

Except when Max had put his hands on her ass and she'd felt the solid length of his erection when he'd pressed against her, and he'd whispered in her ear all the naughty, thrilling things he wanted to do to her, the pulsing need between her thighs had elicited a slow burn of desire in the most shocking of places. Places she wanted him to touch and caress . . . with his hands, his fingers, that sinful tongue of his . . .

"Let's face it," Brielle said, her amused voice bringing Hailey's attention back to the present. "At twenty-six, you're practically a virgin all over again."

Hailey laughed, because her friend's observation was pretty much true. She'd had intercourse once, and she'd given a few blow jobs to said college asshole as well. And that had been nearly five years ago. If it weren't for her vibrator, her vagina would probably have cobwebs.

"And now you've got a drop-dead gorgeous hunk of a guy at your disposal, who is willing and able to deliver the goods, without any strings attached or any emotional entanglements to worry about," Brielle went on with her sales pitch in favor of Hailey having sex again. "He's not asking for forever, so just enjoy the situation and him."

No, she wasn't in love with Max, but Hailey could easily admit he was a man she could fall for if she allowed herself. Hotness aside, he was charming and funny and persuasive. He had a kind side, and even that glimpse of alpha male she'd gotten in the elevator earlier today attracted her. Except the prospect of getting her heart broken at the end of this temporary relationship was a scary one.

"The way I see things, there's no reason you shouldn't take advantage of a fake engagement *with* benefits."

Hailey absently turned the long stem of her empty glass, unable to completely squash that vulnerable part of herself that always put the brakes on her self-confidence when it came to getting naked with a man. "I'm sure I'm nothing like the women he's used to, who don't have to worry about wearing Spanx to keep their muffin tops tucked in and everything else smooth."

"*Hello*," Brielle said, pointing to her own pear-shaped body beneath the flattering dress she wore. "Not once has Kenny ever made me feel less than perfect," she said of the guy she'd been seeing for nearly a year now. "Not every man wants a skinny bitch with sharp hip bones and a flat butt and no cushion for the pushing. You've lost over seventy pounds, Hailey. You do yoga and jog on your treadmill every day. You're healthy and beautiful, and it's time for you to embrace all your curves. Own who you are."

Logically, Hailey knew she was right. Mentally, however, it was a harder hurdle to overcome.

Her friend reached across the table and placed her hand over Hailey's, her touch affectionate and caring. "I just want you to have a man in your life who adores *all* of you, and I know he's out there for you, but you can't let your insecurities hold you back. You make other people happy all the time with your matchmaking business, and you should let yourself be happy, too. Give Max a chance . . . even if it's just for sex," she said with a wicked grin.

Hailey laughed. "I'll try," she promised, and meant it. It was time to get out of her own head.

"Good," Brielle said with a satisfied nod as

her gaze shifted to something behind Hailey, and her eyes lit up with delight. "Well, speak of the handsome devil," she murmured, and a moment later, Hailey found out who had grabbed her friend's attention.

Max came into view and stopped at their table, with a dark-blonde-haired man by his side dressed in a navy blue Premier Realty T-shirt, faded jeans, and work boots. Hailey recognized the other guy as Connor, who worked in the construction side of the business as an investor and property flipper. According to what Max had told her when she'd first met Connor at the office, the company also purchased old homes and buildings that they then remodeled and upgraded and put back on the market for a higher resale value.

"Good evening, ladies," Max said in greeting.

"Hi, guys," Hailey replied politely. Brielle knew Max from the few times in the past when she'd accompanied Hailey to a listing, but since she didn't know Connor, Hailey made the introductions.

"Nice to meet you, Brielle," Connor said, then glanced back at Hailey. "I just wanted to stop by and issue my congratulations. It's not every day that Max gets engaged."

Hailey's mouth opened, then closed again. That was the last thing she'd expected Connor to congratulate her for—her newly acquired property, yes, but oh, my God, did he really believe they were *engaged* engaged? Connor's expression was so serious she couldn't tell if he was joking or not.

She heard Brielle snicker, and she lifted a brow at Max, who looked completely at ease with the situation. "You told him we're *really* engaged?"

He cocked his head, his brownish-green eyes filled with mischief. "Of course I did. Everyone in the office now knows what a lucky guy I am. Didn't you tell Brielle the good news?"

Hailey felt flustered and was certain it showed in her stunned expression. "Of course I did, but she knows the truth. That it's all pretend."

Connor busted out laughing. "Oh, my God, the look on your face is absolutely priceless. No worries, we all know you two are faking it and why."

Hailey groaned. "I take it Max told you the whole humiliating story about our incident with

Maureen?"

"Yeah," Connor said, chuckling. "I just wanted to come by and say hi, but I'm going to head over to the bar to sit with a few of my friends."

Connor said good-bye and left their table, but Max boldly slid into the booth right next Hailey without an invitation, not that she minded. The warm scent of his cologne instantly wrapped around her, and he didn't hesitate to sit close enough that his thigh was pressed against hers—as if they were really a couple. Awareness fluttered inside of her, and while she'd normally try and scoot away from such an intimate gesture, she reminded herself that she'd just promised Brielle that she was going to give Max a chance . . . *even if it was just for sex*, as her friend had said.

Max turned toward Hailey, meeting her gaze with one of his sexy, teasing smiles. "I know this might look like I'm stalking you, but I swear I'm not," he added with a wink at the inside joke only the two of them were a part of. "Connor and I were just coming in for a beer after work. I had no idea you came here, too."

"This is our first time, actually," she told him. "Drinks and appetizers are great."

He glanced at their empty glasses. "Can I get you two another cocktail?"

"Not for me," Brielle said, holding up her hand. "I need to leave soon. I'm meeting my boyfriend in about a half an hour after he gets out of a meeting."

"What does he do?" Max asked, sounding genuinely interested.

"He's an accountant." Brielle casually folded her arms on the table. "The end of March and beginning of April are always long, busy days for him. But the man needs to eat, and I enjoy cooking for him, so we try to spend a few hours a night together."

"Nice." He returned his attention back to Hailey with a warm smile. "By the way, I have a question for you."

"Oh?" she asked curiously.

"There's a small, casual get-together I'm going to this weekend. Do you remember meeting Wes and Natalie at the office?"

She nodded. It had been a while ago, but she recalled meeting them in passing one day when she was at Premier Realty going over a few listings with Max.

"The two of them have been dating for a while. They recently got engaged and moved into a new place together a few weeks ago. They're having a few of us over on Sunday, and I'd like you to come with me."

Hanging out with Max's friends, like a real couple, hadn't been part of their deal. She was about to tell him that she really needed to start packing up her place to move in a month, but he spoke again before the excuse could leave her mouth.

"How about I pick you up around four in the afternoon?" he said, as if it was a foregone conclusion that she was accompanying him. "We can consider it a practice run before my dad's birthday when we *really* have to convince people we're engaged." He grinned at her.

Brielle laughed, the sound rife with amusement, and Hailey was fairly certain that her friend was enjoying this man's confidence and determination when it came to persuading her.

"Oh, I think you're going to be really good for her, Max," Brielle said in a delighted tone.

"Yeah?" he asked, looking intrigued by Brielle's comment. "Why's that?"

Brielle's smile was almost giddy. "Because she needs someone to push her outside of the comfort zone she's boxed herself into for much too long, and I think you're the perfect man for the job."

Hailey felt her cheeks warm from embarrassment, and even though she shot silent daggers at Brielle from across the table to *zip it*, her friend blatantly ignored her glare.

Max flashed one of his flirtatious grins. "Well, in that case, I'll see what I can do."

God, the two were actually conspiring against her! She looked at Brielle with big, meaningful eyes. "Don't you need to leave?"

"Yep," she said happily as she gathered up her purse. "My work here is done. You two behave yourselves."

"Now what's the fun in that?" Max's voice was smooth and deep and full of naughty insinuation.

"So true," Brielle agreed cheerfully. "In that case, don't do anything I wouldn't do, which gives you two a lot of leeway when it comes to all sorts of fun debauchery."

The warmth on Hailey's cheeks started to feel like an inferno. "Go!" she said on a laugh as she pointed to the door.

Brielle slid out of the booth and gave Hailey a finger wave. "See you at the office tomorrow morning."

"Not if I fire you first," she quipped back.

"Pfft." Brielle rolled her eyes loftily. "You love me way too much."

At the moment, that was debatable.

Chapter Five

MAX WATCHED BRIELLE walk away for a moment before he glanced back at Hailey sitting beside him in the booth. Now that her friend—and the buffer between them—was gone and Hailey was alone with him, she was spinning the engagement ring on her finger anxiously. It was something he was starting to notice that she did when she was nervous, which was the last thing he wanted her to be when it was just the two of them.

"Are you okay?" he asked, wanting to make certain that she was fine.

She nodded and gave him a smile he couldn't quite decipher. "I probably should go, and I'm sure you'd like to join Connor over at the bar."

How wrong she was. "Do *you* need to go?"

She blinked in surprise at his question. "Well . . . no."

"Then given the choice, I'd rather be right here with you," he said, and meant it. And since she was still fidgeting with her ring, he gently grabbed her hand, flattened her palm on his thigh, and placed his on top—then immediately tried not to think about how close her fingers were to his dick, because the mental image of her gripping and stroking him would surely lead to his recalcitrant cock getting hard.

Shit, it was probably going to happen anyway, because now that Hailey didn't have her ring to play with, her fingers were starting to flex against his thigh. And fuck, did it feel good, like a sensual massage . . . but it *wasn't*, he reminded himself.

"You need to stop being so nervous with me," he said, rubbing his thumb across her knuckles. "You already know that I don't bite. Much, anyway."

She laughed, and he felt her body relax next to his in subtle degrees. "I'm just not used to . . ."

"A man's sole focus centered around you?" he guessed.

She shrugged and tipped her head forward, causing those silky blonde waves to cover the side of her face. "It's just been awhile."

So he'd gathered from his brief conversation with Brielle. Such a paradox, this woman who ran a successful matchmaking business but didn't seem overly experienced when it came to men and dating.

With his free hand, he pushed her hair back over her shoulder so he could see all of her features again, then touched her chin so that she was looking directly into his eyes. "Just relax and have fun with it, sweetheart. Don't overthink things, okay?"

She nodded and smiled, drawing his gaze to the soft, pink, delectable mouth he couldn't wait to taste again. It had only been a few hours since he'd kissed her at his office, but it already felt like weeks. Their surroundings faded as he dipped his head and leaned in closer, so fucking gratified when her lashes fluttered closed and her lips parted for him . . .

"Can I get either of you anything else to drink or eat?" a waitress asked beside their table, effectively interrupting the kiss.

Startled, Hailey jerked back and tried to tug her hand from his thigh, but he easily held it in place as he casually glanced at the waitress. "I'd like to order the Kobe sliders. I'll also take a Sam Adams on draft." He glanced at Hailey. "Would you like something?"

She looked around him to smile at the waitress. "I'll have a Sprite with lemon, please. That's it for me."

"Nothing to eat?" he asked once the server was gone.

Hailey shook her head. "I'm fine. I shared some stuffed mushrooms with Brielle."

He hoped that wasn't all she planned to have for dinner. He'd noticed at lunch she hadn't finished her meal then, either, but he didn't know her habits well enough—yet—to say anything about them.

She exhaled a breath. "I suppose we should talk about our . . . engagement, and what we're going to tell people when they ask how we met, just so we have our stories straight?"

Entwining her fingers with his, he leaned against the cushion behind him in the booth. "I say we stick as close to the truth as possible so the details are easy to remember. When someone asks how we met, we tell them you were my client looking for a new building to purchase for your business, and it was love at first sight."

He grinned at her.

"Love at first sight?" she repeated, her tone filled with disbelief, but she was smiling. "You just said to stick as close to the truth as possible, and that's pretty farfetched."

"You don't believe in love at first sight? Or are you a more practical girl who relies on compatibility quizzes and all those matchmaking tricks?" Which would make sense, considering her business.

"Compatibility tests do help in terms of finding someone who shares your values, and yes, I do believe love at first sight can happen for some people," she said thoughtfully. "But I've never experienced it for myself."

"Until now," he insisted playfully.

"Okay, okay, until now," she said with a laugh, clearly telling him what he wanted to hear. "With you, of course."

"Good to know we're on the same page with that." He winked at her, enjoying this flirty banter between them.

The waitress came by and delivered their drinks, and once she moved on to another table, he took a long swallow of his beer, then continued with their conversation. "So tell me about your family. You mentioned they lived in

Springfield, right?" Which was about two hundred miles away from Chicago.

"Yes."

"Any brothers or sisters?" he asked, running his fingers along the condensation gathering on his glass.

"No," she said with a shake of her head. "I'm an only child. My parents died in a head-on car accident when I was four, so no siblings."

The faintest hint of sadness tinged her voice, but it was enough that Max felt as though he'd just been punched in the gut. He couldn't imagine how difficult that had been for her as a young child, both emotionally and mentally. "I'm so sorry."

"Thank you." With her straw, she pushed the lime deeper into her glass of Sprite to mix the flavors before taking a quick drink. "Obviously, it was a long time ago, and I was so young. I remember it was difficult for me to understand where my mom and dad were, but as I got older, it all started to seem surreal. Like I never really knew my parents at all."

Their server came back to their table to drop off the appetizer plate Max had ordered, and after making sure they didn't need anything else, she moved on again. Max picked up one of the small hamburgers and continued where they'd left off.

"Who raised you?" he asked curiously, genuinely wanting to know more about her, because everything about her fascinated him.

"My mom's sister and her husband," she told him. "My aunt Sharon and uncle Tony were unable to have children, so I was pretty much it for them." The smile that touched her lips was sentimental. "I also spent a lot of time with both sets of grandparents. My aunt and uncle gave me a great childhood, and there was no doubt in my mind that I was loved, but sometimes, as I got older, it felt as though my aunt, especially, tried to overcompensate for the loss of my parents and losing her own sister."

He swallowed a bite of his sandwich, and suspecting there was something more to her story, he prompted her for more details. "How so?"

Hailey hesitated a few long seconds, debating on whether to share *more* with Max. It was huge that she'd told him about her parents' death and how she'd grown up, which she normally kept to herself with the men she dated because it was so personal. Then again, none of them had ever asked about her past or coaxed her to open up and talk about herself.

One glance into Max's gorgeous eyes and she knew if she wanted to end the direction their discussion was quickly veering off toward, he'd back off and respect her decision. Yeah, that would be the safe bet, but a small part of her wanted to do something completely crazy . . . like trust him.

She'd known this man for three months now, and he'd never given her any indication that he'd judge or criticize her, and she couldn't say that about a lot of the other men she'd dated. Hell, she'd put him through the wringer today, and while most guys would have been pissed that she'd dragged them into her farce without their knowledge, what did Max do? He'd not only played along like a pro in front of Maureen but he'd agreed to step in and pose as her loving fiancé.

Yes, he was getting something out of the charade, as well, but his actions today just affirmed the chivalrous kind of guy that he was. And if she really wanted to enjoy her time with Max without constantly feeling self-conscious, then he needed to know the truth about her past so he could better understand her hesitation when it came to *negotiating* any other physical intimacy with him beyond kissing.

She exhaled a slow, deep breath, but when she remained fidgety and nervous, she automatically tried to pull her fingers out of his grasp so she could calm herself by turning her ring.

He held on tight, refusing to let go. "Hailey . . . whatever it is, I've got you," he said softly.

Ahhh, such a simple comment that meant so much. He was asking her to trust him, and he was holding her hand as if *he* were her anchor, her pillar of support. But most importantly, she *believed* him.

She wasn't a theatrical person, but his caring display was enough to make a girl swoon. And it gave her the fortitude to share one of her deepest vulnerabilities with him. He wanted to know how her aunt tried to make up for the loss of Hailey's parents, and she told him.

"As I said, I always felt loved, but as I was growing up, my aunt Sharon would always buy me elaborate things I didn't need, and the older I got, the more I realized how excessive it all was. Also, from the time I started living with them, whenever I was feeling down or sad about my parents, my aunt would bake things that she would encourage me to eat. It was as if that was her way of making sure that I felt loved, and in the moment, the cookies, cakes, and brownies *did* feel comforting."

Admitting something that was so hard for her to dredge up made her chest tighten almost painfully. Yet it was the understanding in his eyes and the hand holding hers so securely that gave her the fortitude she needed to keep going.

"Instead of my aunt talking to me about my feelings or discussing how my parents' deaths might have affected me, she'd bring out the desserts to cheer me up and make me feel better," she said, her voice a bit rough around the edges. "And because that's all I knew, eating sweets became my coping mechanism when it came to dealing with my emotions. Except in the long run, it hurt me more than helped me. By the time I graduated from high school, I was considered obese and I'd never been on a date with a guy."

He looked surprised—not repulsed as she'd feared. "You certainly aren't obese now."

Neither was she slender and lithe, and beneath her clothes, the evidence of that extra weight remained in places. "When my parents died, they both had a substantial life insurance policy, and my aunt and uncle put it all into a trust, which they gave to me when I graduated. As much as I loved my aunt and uncle, I knew I needed to find myself, and I registered for college at University of Chicago. It was close enough that I could go home if I needed to but far enough away that I could live my own life."

"And did you find yourself?" he asked with a smile.

She laughed easily, appreciating him keeping things light. "Actually, yes I did. It was quite liberating being out on my own. My freshman year, I went to a nutritionist, who put me on a meal and diet plan, and after a year, I'd lost seventy pounds."

"That's impressive and a huge accomplishment," he said as he went back to eating the last small hamburger on his plate, then frowned as he was swallowing the bite. "You're not starving yourself, are you? You didn't eat all your lunch today, and you had mushrooms for dinner."

"I'm fine," she insisted, a little shocked that he'd even noticed and that he was concerned that she wasn't depriving herself. "There's something else I still need to tell you."

"Okay," he said, his attention back on her.

Her nerves made her throat feel dry, and she

took a drink of her Sprite while telling herself that she'd already come this far, and she needed to finish the story. "So, by my junior year and having lost so much weight, Brielle convinced me to start dating, and when a guy in my biology class asked me out, I said yes."

She automatically glanced away from Max's intense gaze and pressed her free hand to her churning stomach. Just thinking about that memory still had the ability to make her cheeks heat with mortification.

"Hailey, look at me."

Max's voice was soft yet commanding, and she did as he asked and turned her head back toward him, her eyes reluctantly meeting his.

The gentle and kind look in his gaze helped to alleviate the turmoil in her belly. "Whatever happened, whatever you're going to tell me, I'm not going to think any less of you."

It was so easy to lower her guard with him, to feel safe sharing her secrets, because she believed what he said. He wouldn't still be sitting beside her if he was the type of guy who was all about a woman's physical appearance. "After a few dates, we ended up sleeping together. He was the first guy I'd ever had sex with, and the next day, he sent me a text message ending the relationship because he wasn't into fat chicks."

Max's jaw clenched and his eyes flashed with anger. "Fucking asshole."

He was so vehement on her behalf she couldn't help but smile. "Yeah, tact obviously wasn't his forte," she agreed, then turned serious again. "The thing is . . . I haven't been with a man since, and that was almost five years ago."

He frowned slightly, and she could see him processing that statement. "Wait. You're a professional matchmaker, and you can't find a man you're compatible with enough to date?" His tone was incredulous.

She knew how crazy it sounded, given her profession, and tried to explain what she'd meant. "It has nothing to do with being compatible with a guy, and yes, I've *dated* since that incident in college." The next part was more difficult to reveal, and with a *go big or go home* attitude, she forced it out. "I just haven't *slept* with anyone since because, well, I'm . . . nervous. And afraid of being humiliated again," she admitted on a rush, laying her insecurities out on the table. "It's my hang-up, obviously, and most men don't have the patience to deal with my insecurities, not that I can blame them, so my relationships are fairly short-lived."

Max studied her for a long, thoughtful moment. "Do you *want* to have sex again?"

She laughed and shook her head, unable to believe that they were having such a frank discussion about her sex life. "Yes, I'd like to have sex again." She wasn't a prude, just . . . apprehensive about putting herself out there again on a physical level. "It would help if I could just get out of my head and not panic when things start to go in that direction."

"Then we'll take it slow," he said, his voice low and sexy as he reached out with his free hand and trailed his fingers along her jaw. "I like you, Hailey, and now that I know there's not another guy in the picture, fuck yeah I want to sleep with you, because I'm attracted to you." He skimmed his thumb across her bottom lip, his gaze darkening with heat and desire. "But I'll never pressure you for something you don't want or you're not ready to give me. When it happens, it's going to be because you fucking beg for it. Understand?"

Hailey's breath seemed to vanish from her lungs as her body responded to his explicit words. The fact that he sounded so confident of his ability to make her *fucking beg for it* made her toes curl in her pumps and her nipples tighten into hard, aching points. Her panties felt damp, and the flesh between her legs pulsed with need.

"Yes, I understand," she said, barely recognizing her own husky voice.

"Perfect." A seductive smile curved his lips as his gaze dropped to her mouth. "I can't wait to hear you beg," he said oh-so-confidently.

Hailey shivered, but before she could respond to that promise, the waitress stopped by their table to clear Max's empty plate. "Do either of you want or need anything else before I bring the check?"

"No, thank you," Hailey said.

Max shook his head. "I'm good."

"Then I'll be right back with the bill," the server said.

Hailey glanced at the time on her phone, surprised to see that it was already past eight in the evening. "I really should get going. I have an early meeting with a client tomorrow morning who is having her first matchmaking reception on Saturday."

"Sure." Max withdrew his wallet and paid the bill when it was delivered, then moved out of the booth so she could slide out, too. "I'll walk you out to your car."

"You don't need to do that," she said, putting on the sweater she'd worn to the restaurant since it was the beginning of April and still chilly outside in the evenings. "Since you spent all your time with me tonight, you should probably go and hang out with Connor for a bit."

"I know I don't *need* to do it," Max replied with lighthearted sarcasm as he grabbed her hand again—something she secretly liked and was quickly getting used to. "I *want* to do it. And even if I did plan to join Connor, I'm not letting you walk to your car alone at night."

Always the gentleman, of course Max would insist on accompanying her. She didn't issue any other argument as he headed toward the front of the restaurant. The last time he'd held her hand like this, he'd been dragging her back to his office for a confrontation, with her trotting a few steps behind him because of his fast stride. This time, she was able to walk next to Max, like they were a couple, and when a few single women sitting at the bar glanced at Max appreciatively, a territorial thought popped into her mind.

Back off, ladies. He's mine. Or at least he

would be for a little while, until she figured a way out of this mess she'd gotten them both into. The end was inevitable. It was just a matter of when. Max himself had admitted to being a bachelor, and she wasn't foolish enough to believe she'd be the one to change that status.

Her car was parked to the side of the building, and when they neared her white Honda Accord, she disengaged the alarm and unlocked the door with her remote. Max walked her to the driver's side, but instead of opening the door, he turned her around and gently eased her backside against the side of the vehicle.

As soon as her body touched the car, she sucked in a quick breath. "The metal is cold."

He smirked and didn't hesitate to align his body right in front of hers, making her want to snuggle into the delicious heat emanating off of him. "Then it's a good thing I'm here to warm you up."

She laughed, and now that everything was out in the open between them, it was easy for Hailey to relax and enjoy what she knew was about to happen. Want it, even. Because kissing Max was one of the most singularly pleasant things she'd ever experienced, and she wasn't about to pass up the opportunity to do it again.

He pushed his hands into her hair, his fingers tugging on the strands as he tipped her head back and looked into her eyes with a smile that was as sensual as a caress. "So, how would you like this kiss, sweet girl?" he murmured, the rich timbre of his voice flowing over her like warm honey. "Slow and soft and all about the romance? Or hard and deep and thorough?"

She'd already experienced both with Max, and either option made her blood sing, but the thought of him seducing her mouth and taking his time doing it already had her legs quivering. "I want it slow, please," she whispered.

"Good choice," he said, dipping his head to lick across her bottom lip before sealing their mouths together, giving her what she asked for, everything she craved with him.

He took his time and didn't rush, making sure her lips were nice and wet and slick before he took things deeper. She moaned when he slid his tongue inside, her hands reaching out and settling at his sides, just above the waistband of his dress pants. She could feel the heat of his skin through his shirt, and if she were braver and more sexually daring, she would have pulled the hem from his trousers so she could run her fingers over his firm stomach and up to his chest.

As if he had all night long, his tongue stroked lazily along hers, lingering and teasing and tempting her as he slanted her head one way, then another, depending on the angle he wanted. Her breasts tightened and ached, and she moved restlessly against him, drawing a groan from his chest that reverberated against her lips.

After what seemed like forever, he moved his mouth from hers. He slid his lips along her jaw, trailing soft, gentle kisses up to her ear while pressing his hips harder against hers. "Can you feel how much I want you?" he asked, his breath hot and damp on her neck.

He was at least seven solid inches of wanting her, and her sex clenched at the thought of him filling her and burying the rigid length of his cock to the hilt so that she was completely pinned beneath him. "Oh, God, yes."

She felt him smile against her neck before he marked her with a gentle love bite that sent tremors running throughout her body. "When you're ready, when you're begging for my cock, it's yours," he said with a rough edge to his voice. "*All* of it. As hard and deep as you want it. As fast as you need it."

A soft, mewling sound rose up from her throat—a sound so shameless it shocked her. She was slick between her thighs, so *physically* ready she knew it wouldn't take much to orgasm if she were at home, lying in her bed, her fingers circling and rubbing her clit. No man had ever given her an orgasm—by hand, mouth, or intercourse—and she suddenly wanted Max to be the first to make her climax, when that time came. And she knew without a doubt, sooner or later it was going to happen, because she *wanted* it to.

Max finally lifted his head from her neck, his breathing harsh as he stared into her eyes. "Jesus," he rasped, the sound scratchy and aroused. "All I can say is that any man you've ever dated has been stupid as fuck. And they obviously don't know what to do with a woman as sexy and passionate as you." A slow, sinful smile curved his mouth. "But don't worry, sweet girl, I know exactly what to do to make your body purr."

She bit her bottom lip, believing every word he spoke.

He gently released her hair and slowly took a step back. Then, he opened the car door for her and waited until she was in the leather seat and buckled up before saying, "So, I'll pick you up at four on Sunday for the get-together at Wes and Natalie's?"

"Yes," she said, looking forward to seeing him again.

"See you then," he replied with a smile as he closed her door.

God, three days never felt so far away in her life.

Chapter Six

A T TEN THIRTY on Friday evening, Max lay in bed watching an episode of *Criminal Minds* on TV, debating on whether or not to call Hailey. Deliberately not contacting her for the past twenty-four hours since he'd put her inside her car and she'd driven away from him had been sheer torture. He'd been restless all day, finding it hard to concentrate when his mind was consumed with thoughts of her and everything that had transpired between them the day before.

In the span of a few hours, they'd gone from business associates to perpetuating a fake engagement, not that he was complaining about the legitimate excuse he now had to spend more time with her. He'd been attracted to Hailey from the first day they'd met, and the more he learned about her, the more his interest increased, not diminished as it normally did with the women he'd dated in the past—or with the women his mother set him up with.

While all those other women had been beautiful and sophisticated and worldly, they'd lacked . . . substance. In comparison to Hailey, their conversations were superficial, their personalities one-dimensional and shallow. The topic of discussion was either all about them or they tried too hard to impress him. He'd been through the same process, time and again. Different women but the same end result of being bored and his interest quickly waning.

Coming from a wealthy family, and having done extremely well in the luxury real estate business, Max knew his money was definitely an allure to the fairer sex. But at the age of thirty, he was at a point in his life where he was looking for more in a relationship. He wanted something substantial and meaningful, and a connection that went deeper than just surface appearances or a temporary hookup. Hailey had given him a glimpse of all those things last night at the bar, when she'd opened up and shared something so personal and private with him—

her parents' deaths, being raised by her aunt and uncle, and her struggle to be on her own and make positive changes in her life. But he'd also been privy to a deeply vulnerable side to Hailey that had stirred his protective instincts, and that was something new to him, too. If he ever came across the asshole who'd damaged her self-esteem in college, Max was certain the other man wouldn't walk away unscathed. In fact, he'd take great pleasure in teaching the jerk some manners—with his fist, because Max was all about defending a woman's honor.

The TV show he was barely paying attention to went to commercial, and he reached over to his nightstand and picked up his cell phone. After everything that had happened yesterday, he'd wanted to give Hailey space so she didn't feel overwhelmed—by their real fake engagement or by him. But as he was starting to learn Hailey's habits and understand her insecurities, he was concerned that time apart for three days, without any contact, might cause her to doubt *them*, which in turn would make things awkward between them when they saw each other again on Sunday. And that was the last thing he wanted.

Decision made, he put the TV on mute and

hooked up his Bluetooth so he could be hands-free, then brought up her number and put the call through. This was all about making sure she knew he was thinking of her, and he planned on keeping their conversation easy and casual. Nothing heavy or deep, especially after last night's emotional revelations.

He set his phone beside him on the bed and relaxed more fully against the pillows he'd stacked behind him as she answered the call.

"Max?" she said, her husky voice drifting through the line. "Is everything okay?"

He heard the concern lacing her question, and realizing that the late hour must have worried her, he was quick with a reassurance. "Everything is fine. Did I wake you?" He cringed. He should have thought about that possibility before he'd called, considering it was now nearly ten forty-five.

"No. I'm in bed, but I'm still up," she said with a soft sigh, the seductive sound making his cock twitch beneath the cotton fabric of his boxer briefs. "I always find it hard to sleep the night before a matchmaking event since I've got so many things going through my head that I don't want to forget. It's hard for my brain to shut down." She paused, then asked self-consciously, "Is there something you needed?"

"No." He smiled to himself. "I just wanted to hear your voice and see how your day was."

"Oh." He heard her surprise, as if she wasn't used to someone checking up on her. "It was good but busy. Yours?"

"Same," he said, wondering if he ought to let her go back to bed, considering her long day tomorrow. "Do you want me to let you go so you can try and sleep?"

"No," she said quickly, leaving no doubt in his mind that she was staying on the phone because she wanted to. "You're a nice distraction and I like talking to you."

Her admission pleased him, and since he wanted to keep things light and playful, he came up with an idea. "Speaking of distractions . . . want to play a game?"

Her soft, sexy laughter was like a silky stroke across his skin. "Depends on the game. I think I'm beginning to realize that you like things a little . . . dirty."

She was being a bit bolder than normal, probably because she didn't have to look him in the eyes, and the safety of being on opposite ends of the line made her willing to take a few risks. To be a little naughty and flirt, and he intended to take advantage of her relaxed mood.

He clasped his hands on his bare stomach and settled in. "You don't seem to mind me being dirty when I'm whispering in your ear all the filthy things I want to do to you."

"Is that your game?" she murmured, a smile in her voice. "Who can talk the dirtiest? Because if so, you'll win, hands down."

"Don't worry, we'll work on that." Because, yeah, he was looking forward to hearing that sweet mouth of hers telling him exactly what her body wanted, in explicit terms. "You just need a bit more practice talking dirty to someone who likes it. That would be me."

She laughed again, amused this time. "What is the game, Max?"

"It's called ask me anything," he told her, tongue-in-cheek. "Since we're still in the getting-to-know-you stage of our engagement, I figure it'll help us get better acquainted with each other so we're prepared for any personal questions when you meet my family. I'll start."

"Okay."

He began with a simple, basic one. "Which would you rather have in the morning . . ." *Warm, sleepy sex in bed or a hot, slippery fuck in the shower?* was what he *wanted* to ask. Instead, he went with a much safer, "Coffee or tea?"

"Definitely coffee," she replied easily. "With cream and sugar. I can't start the day without caffeine. You?"

"Coffee. Strong and black," he replied. "Now it's your turn to ask me something."

"Hmmm." The line went quiet for a few seconds while she thought about her question. "Do you prefer watching movies or reading books?"

"Watching movies," he said without hesitation. "I'm all about instant gratification."

"Of course you are," she said wryly, and he imagined her doing an exaggerated eye roll. "I prefer reading. I'm all about making it *last.*"

He chuckled, enjoying the fact that she was comfortable enough to tease him and issue sexual innuendos. They spent the next half an hour asking most of the basic questions couples would want to know about each other: favorite color, favorite thing to do for fun, their major in college, favorite foods, and at least a dozen other common queries that gave them both better insight into their lives and personalities.

"What is your most annoying quirk?" Hailey asked when it was her turn again.

He groaned. "Are you really going to make me admit my worst habit so soon?"

"Yes," she said, laughing.

"What if there's more than one?" He certainly wasn't a saint.

"Then I think you're obligated to divulge the truth to your fiancée," she said playfully. "I need to know what I'm getting myself into."

"Fair enough." He mentally pulled up a list of all those traits that would undoubtedly drive a woman nuts, and prepared himself to man up. "Let's see . . . I drink orange juice out of the carton, but in my defense, I live alone, so it's not as though anyone else is drinking it. I also let the dishes in the sink pile up, but I do rinse them first. If I'm watching a baseball game on TV, nothing else outside my personal bubble exists, and if you touch the remote or change the channel during the game, you will pay dearly. Yes, I leave the toilet seat up, but I'm sure I can be trained to put it down when I'm done. I occasionally leave wet towels on the bathroom floor and . . . can I stop now, please?" he all but begged, laughing.

"Wow." She sounded completely shocked that he'd actually confessed all his transgressions. "I didn't expect you to be so . . . honest."

He smirked as he absently scratched a spot on his belly. "I'm not going to ask if *you* have any irritating habits, because I'm still in the honeymoon phase of our relationship, but I think you owe me big-time for that question and, of course, my honest answers."

"You'd better make it a good one then."

Damn. Was that a sultry *dare* he detected in her voice? He believed it was, and he wasn't about to back down from her inviting challenge.

"What is your hottest sexual fantasy?" he asked, going for the gusto. "When you're in bed at night, touching yourself, what gets you off?"

A long stretch of silence ensued, and he was almost certain he heard crickets chirping across the phone line. He gave her time to absorb his request, to gather the confidence to tell him what he wanted to hear.

"Umm." Her nervous hesitation vibrated against the Bluetooth piece in his ear. "I'm not sure that's a question that your family is going to ask me."

He laughed at her comment, which was a blatant attempt at avoidance. "I sure hope the fuck not. This question, and your answer, is all for me, sweet girl."

He heard her exhale a deep breath, still uncertain, and decided to give her a little nudge in the right direction. "Are you still in bed?"

A distinct pause, then, "Yes."

"Good," he murmured gently. "Now close your eyes, relax your entire body, and imagine me kissing your neck and gradually sliding my lips down to your gorgeous breasts. Your nipples are already hard for me, aren't they, sweetheart? So tight they want to be sucked on, and gently bitten."

"Yes," she said, an unmistakable tremor in her voice.

He closed his eyes, as well, his own mind getting in on the action as he mentally put himself in Hailey's bed with her and envisioned pushing her tits together, his lips pulling on her tight nipples, his teeth scraping across the rigid tips. His dick hardened to granite, bulging against the front of his boxer briefs. He rubbed his hand over the pulsing length, already aching for release.

"Now spread your legs nice and wide and slide your hand in between," he ordered and knew she'd obeyed when a soft, mewling sound escaped her. "Are you wet?"

"I'm . . . I'm getting there," she admitted self-consciously, and he could easily imagine her blushing, torn between modesty and allowing herself to just let go and lose herself in the fantasy.

"Let me help you get there faster," he offered, knowing he was about to risk pushing her outside that comfort zone Brielle had mentioned. The question was, would she trust him enough to take the leap?

"How?" she rasped in his ear.

"By going down on you and licking your pussy," he said, pushing that vivid image into her mind, and fuck, he wished it were reality. "By sliding my tongue nice and slow through your slit, again and again, then latching onto your clit and sucking until your entire body is shaking with the need to come."

Her breathing hitched. "Oh, God, Max . . . "

"Did that help you get wet?" he asked, his voice sounding as rough as gravel.

"Yes," she said on a moan that told him just how aroused she was.

He coaxed her a little further, pushing her beyond any embarrassment that might still be holding her back. "Use your fingers and tell me what your pussy feels like. Here's your chance to practice a little dirty talk, sweetheart."

Her husky laugh coalesced into a shivery

groan of desire, and there wasn't a doubt in Max's mind that her fingers were slipping and sliding through all that slick, sensitive flesh, possibly even finding their way deeper inside, where he wanted his cock to be. He imagined her spread out naked on her bed, her blonde hair streaming across her pillow and down to her breasts, and the rest of her luscious curves on display as she arched into her own touch.

"Tell me, Hailey," he demanded impatiently.

A needy whimper fell from her lips. "It feels soft . . . warm . . . swollen . . . and so, so wet."

"Jesus. You're so ready for me." He shoved his briefs down to his thighs and wrapped his fingers tight around his cock, squeezing and tugging the thick length in his fist. "I'm so fucking hard and aching. I'm dying to be inside you and feel for myself how soft and warm you are. Do you want that, too?"

"Yes . . . so much," she confessed, her voice infused with the same lust charging through his veins.

"How do you want to be fucked, Hailey?" he rasped, gripping his dick harder and using the bead of pre-cum seeping from the head of his shaft to lubricate his quickening strokes. He was desperate to know what she envisioned while her fingers dipped and swirled and plied her pussy. "Do you want me on top, pinning you down and thrusting into you? Or do you want to ride me so you can grind against my cock? Or would you like me to put you on your hand and knees and wrap your beautiful hair around my fist while I'm taking you from behind? What's that filthy fantasy that gets you off? Tell me, and I'll give it to you."

She was panting now, undeniably aroused. "I want you sitting on a chair and me straddling your hips, our bodies pressed together," she said, sounding lost in the fantasy that went through her mind when she was all alone and pleasuring herself. "I want you hard and deep, with your hands pulling my hair and your mouth on my neck . . . "

Her words trailed off on a moan, clearly consumed by her escalating climax. His was fast approaching. His hand jerked harder, faster, his stomach muscles tightening as he heard the rustling of the sheets on her end as she writhed on her bed and pushed herself toward orgasm.

"Max . . . it feels so good," she moaned, sounding as though she was in her own little universe of bliss, as she imagined him fucking her the way she'd just described to him.

"Then let go and come for me, Hailey," he commanded, and as soon as her soft cries of ecstasy reached his ears—which he decided was flat-out one of the sexiest sounds *ever*—he increased the rhythm of his pumping hand and finally allowed the tension gathering in his balls to release.

He growled deep in his throat as a sharp, powerful climax ripped through him. His heartbeat pounded in his chest as he quickly jacked the head of his cock, causing his orgasm to jet against his taut belly—hot and thick and utterly satisfying.

Jesus fucking Christ. He was gasping like he'd just finished a marathon. He collapsed back against his pillows, and it took him a few extra seconds to gain his bearings. When he did, he noticed how quiet it was, but as he listened a little harder, he definitely heard Hailey's soft, erratic breathing on the other end of the line.

He reached over to the nightstand, grabbed a few tissues, and cleaned up the mess he'd made on his stomach. "Hey, you okay over there?" he asked, the Bluetooth still secure in his ear.

"I . . . umm . . ." She cleared her throat and tried again, but her voice remained flustered. "I can't believe that I . . . that we just did that."

He could easily picture that adorable rosy hue of embarrassment flushing across her cheeks, down her neck, and across her breasts. "Any regrets?" He'd been the one to instigate the phone sex and coaxed her to join in. Had he pushed her too far too fast?

"No," she said, much to his relief. "I'm just . . . shocked, but not in a bad way."

He grinned as he pulled his boxer briefs back up to his hips. "You did good for your first session of dirty talk. Definitely an A-plus."

She groaned in mortification, the sound muffled, as if she was covering her face with her hands. "I can't believe the things that came out of my mouth."

And he'd loved every single second of it. "It was so fucking hot. Best part? Now I know what your go-to fantasy is." Actually, he was pretty sure it was forever engraved in his brain.

"Not fair," she murmured, sounding completely relaxed and content. "I don't know what yours is."

He chuckled, happy enough that she *wanted* to hear what turned him on. "How about we save that for another night?"

"Good idea." She yawned drowsily and

made a soft humming noise in the back of her throat. "I think I'm ready to fall asleep now."

"Yeah, a good orgasm is the best sleep aid there is," he teased her with a smile. "I'm so happy I could be of assistance."

"Me, too," she admitted with a touch of humor in her voice. "Good night, Max."

"Good night, sweet girl."

The line disconnected, and Max remained right where he was for a few extra minutes, his own body sated and replete. Eventually, he removed his earpiece, went to the bathroom to better clean himself, then crawled back into bed, his mind playing over everything that had just happened.

When he'd decided to call her tonight, he'd never anticipated that their conversation would turn sexual. That hadn't been his intention, but when she'd tempted him to *make his question a good one*, he hadn't been able to resist. He figured she would either shut him down or she'd play along. He'd had nothing to lose, really.

When she'd leaned toward the latter, it had been so easy to persuade and seduce her into giving him what he wanted—though he knew her willingness to talk dirty and touch herself so uninhibitedly was probably because they hadn't been in the same room together. That way, he couldn't look at her naked body, couldn't watch her slide her fingers between her spread legs, and he couldn't see everything she was so used to hiding from a man because of her insecurities.

That sense of obscurity had made her feel safe, secure, and less vulnerable. Being in separate bedrooms miles apart, there was no issue of her being nervous or self-conscious, nothing to hinder her enjoyment of some hot and heavy phone sex and a mind-blowing orgasm to go with it. She'd been bold and daring and sexy as fuck, and as a bonus, he'd learned some valuable information about her sexual preferences, which he intended to use in the future, when he knew for certain that she was ready to take that next intimate step with him. Knowing her fantasy of choice would give him the leverage he'd need to seduce her when the time came.

He smiled to himself, satisfied with their progress for now. Having sex with Hailey wasn't about rushing the process and fucking her just because he was horny and needed to get off. With her, it was all about building intimacy and trust between them and making sure she knew, without a doubt, his desire for her was real and *everything* about her turned him on.

Tonight was definitely a start.

✧   ✧   ✧

SWEET OR SALTY?

Hailey read Max's brief text as she sat in her current small office Saturday afternoon, unable to hold back the grin playing across her lips. And why would she want to repress it, anyway? All day long, he'd been sending her random questions, continuing where last night's getting-to-know-you game had left off. Well, sort of. Their Q and A session had definitely taken a path she'd never seen coming, from her innocently asking Max what his worst habit was to him responding with an explicit *what is your hottest sexual fantasy?*

She leaned back in her chair and didn't even bother to hide the delicious shiver that accompanied the erotic memories that came *after* that question. God, if Max could make her come as hard as she had with nothing but filthy words, then she could only imagine what kind of pleasure she'd experience if they were in the same room together, with him actually *doing* everything she'd fantasized about.

Sweet or salty. Hmmm. That simple question could be taken a number of ways, and considering that some of Max's texts had *implied* something more sexual, she wasn't sure how to take this one.

She typed back, *Depends on what we're talking about here.*

Get your mind out of the gutter, sweetheart, he responded right away.

She bit her bottom lip, enjoying the playful banter. *What? It's a legitimate question.*

A line of bubbles displayed across her phone screen as he typed a response. *I think I've created a monster. One night of dirty phone sex and you turn everything I ask into an innuendo.*

She laughed. *I do not!*

Ha! When I asked you earlier today what things stimulate you, your answer was hardly innocent, Ms. Ellison.

Grinning like a fool, her fingers tapped across the keyboard, and she hit send. *What? A vibrator is stimulating.*

I meant intellectually, *you bad girl. Maybe you'd find a spanking equally stimulating.* He followed that up with a smirking devil emoticon.

Maybe I would, she replied automatically, and her eyes widened as she prematurely hit the send button. God, had she really just said that? Yes, yes, she had, because it was so easy to be a little shameless with him through texts.

He was quick to reply. *That's what happens to bad girls. Spankings. And other fun stuff.* He included a winky face. *Now back to my original question. Sweet or salty* foods? *How's that for being specific?*

She could almost hear the playful sarcasm in that last question. *Well, there's no misunderstanding what you're asking. And it's definitely sweet. Desserts are my weakness.*

I'd have to go with salty. I'm a chips and nuts kind of guy. And just to clarify, by nuts, I mean almonds and cashews.

She burst out laughing. *See? You're the one with all the innuendos.*

I have no idea what you're talking about. An angel emoticon popped onto the screen. *Next question, and this is an important one. Whipped cream or chocolate sauce to go with your cherry?*

She rolled her eyes at his obvious innuendo and decided to be a little naughty and play along. *I really like both whipped cream and chocolate sauce with my cherry. Why can't I have both?*

Greedy girl. You can have both the whipped cream and the chocolate sauce . . . as long as I get to eat your cherry. I think that's more than fair.

She groaned quietly and pressed her thighs together to subdue the sudden pulsing ache in between. He was so indecent; she couldn't deny that she loved flirting with him. He made her feel sexy and beautiful and desirable, and that was something that had always been lacking with other men she'd dated.

Her phone pinged with another text from him. *FYI. The chocolate sauce and whipped cream will be arriving later.*

A wicked reply popped into her head, and before she could change her mind, she typed it out and dispatched the message. *Only if it comes with you.*

Fuck. If I didn't know you were so busy this afternoon and evening with your matchmaking reception, I would definitely deliver it in person so I could watch you enjoy both. Just remember, your cherry is mine.

She shivered and touched the pulse beating rapidly at the base of her throat. God, this man was so intoxicating, in every way, and he was making it so difficult to not only resist him but to keep her heart and emotions out of this fake engagement.

A knock on her office door startled Hailey, and as if she'd just been caught watching porn, she quickly placed her phone with the screen side down on her desk and stared at Brielle with wide eyes that no doubt disclosed a guilty expression.

Brielle sauntered into the room carrying a plant, her gaze narrowing suspiciously as she glanced from Hailey's hand covering her cell phone to her flaming-hot cheeks. "Why is your face so pink?" she asked suspiciously.

"Umm, it's just warm in here," she fibbed. Brielle knew nothing about her phone-sex session with Max last night, and she wasn't about to reveal their naughty texts, either.

But Brielle was always perceptive when it came to her, and as her friend approached Hailey's desk, a knowing smirk gradually tipped up the corners of her mouth. "You hiding something on your phone, Hailey?"

Knowing Brielle wouldn't let up until she got the info she wanted, Hailey shrugged and kept her reply casual. "It's just a text from Max."

"Ahhh, hot, sexy, hunky Max," she said, her tone playful. "Well, whatever he had to say, it looks like it made you a little hot and bothered. I approve."

Hailey rolled her eyes and stood, her gaze focusing on the pretty ceramic pot Brielle had just set on her desk that contained a gorgeous array of bright purple Phalaenopsis orchids blooming from the ends of their long stems—her favorite flower. She immediately knew who they were from, even before she pulled the attached card from its envelope and read the note Max had written inside.

When I texted you this morning to ask you roses or tulips, I should have known that your answer wouldn't be the normal, typical flower that most women desire. You're as unique and beautiful as these orchids are. Max

The pleasure and giddy joy that filled Hailey were indescribable. Her stomach felt as though a dozen butterflies had taken flight inside, and she couldn't contain the delighted smile she knew was spread across her face.

Standing beside her—and having shamelessly read the note, too—Brielle sighed wistfully. "That's *so* sweet and romantic."

Hailey reached out and touched one of the purple flowers, which was also her favorite color—something else Max had asked her earlier. The orchids were delicate and elegant yet sturdy, their petals velvet soft against the pad of her finger. Yes, she'd told him she loved orchids. Clearly, he paid attention to her answers, and the fact that he'd done something so spontaneous and thoughtful, just because he could, made her feel special and adored. Two things that she didn't have a whole lot of experience with.

"Stop overanalyzing things," Brielle said knowingly as she looped her arm through Hailey's. "Just enjoy the attention. And Max."

Max had told her pretty much the same thing the night at the bar, and she appreciated the reminder from her best friend. "I will."

"Good." Brielle released her and stepped back. "By the way, we need to leave in about forty minutes to head to Acadia to get everything set up for tonight's matchmaking reception for Diane Franklin."

Acadia was the restaurant they currently used for their agency events since they had a large private room Hailey could rent out for the evening, along with great appetizers and drinks for her clients. As soon as she moved into her new building, she planned to redecorate the entire second floor to use to host various events for their clients.

"Okay. Just let me finish a few things in my office, and I'll be ready to go."

"I'll gather up the name tags and icebreaker

games to take with us," Brielle said as she headed out of the office.

Once she was gone, Hailey picked up her cell phone again, wincing when she read the last message from Max, which made her realize she'd left him hanging at a crucial part of their conversation.

Hello? Did I go too far with that cherry comment? He added a smiling emoticon to his text.

She grinned and quickly replied. *No, not considering how far we went last night, LOL. By the way, the flowers are beautiful. Thank you.*

You're welcome. Before you go . . . what color panties are you wearing?

She bit back a grin, no longer shocked by his getting-to-know-you questions. He was gradually stripping away her inhibitions, making it increasingly easier for her to just indulge and enjoy their attraction, and she was fairly certain that was his intent. Mission accomplished.

Light pink, she answered.

Silk or cotton?

She wished she could say silk, just because she knew the mental image was sexier, but she replied honestly. *Cotton with lace trim.* She was a practical girl when it came to her underwear.

Ummm. Pretty. Will you show them to me some-

time? While you're still wearing them?

At the provocative image of her lifting her dress to give him a glimpse of her panties and his gaze darkening as he watched, heated desire bloomed in her belly and made its way between her thighs. *You're such a naughty boy, Max Sterling.*

His answer took a few extra seconds to come through. *After last night, there shouldn't be a single doubt in your mind just how naughty, dirty, and filthy I can get. And judging by the end result to our phone-sex session, which would be you coming for me, I'm inclined to believe you like me that way.*

It was hard to argue his point. Even now, after reading that text and recalling her body's response to his erotic commands the night before, her breasts were tight and her nipples hard. *I do like you that way.* Her finger hovered over the send button as she realized what her reply would reveal—that she was starting to trust him more intimately. She exhaled a deep breath and forwarded the text, and before he could say anything else, she quickly sent another message. *I have to go. We're leaving for the match-making event soon.*

Much to her relief, he didn't pursue her "I do like you that way" comment, and instead replied to the latter remark.

I hope everything goes well tonight, and I'll pick you up at your place at four tomorrow afternoon. The get-together is just a few of us and super-casual, so dress comfortably.

The thought of seeing him again brought back that rush of excitement and gave her something to look forward to, instead of spending another Sunday on her own. *Okay, see you then.*

Chapter Seven

MAX SAT AT a large dining table with his Premier Realty partners, who were also his best friends, as they drank a beer and bullshitted back and forth while Natalie and Hailey were in the kitchen doing their thing. They'd already gotten the grand tour of Wes and Natalie's house—a sprawling one-story that Kyle and Connor had helped to renovate before they'd moved in, and Max had to admit that the place was impressive.

From top to bottom, the entire house had been renovated and modernized, with new hardwood floors, crown molding, paint, upgraded hardware, and a gourmet kitchen with all the bells and whistles. Walls had been knocked down to give the house an open-concept design, and rooms had been restructured, one of which Natalie had turned into an insanely large closet, with floor-to-ceiling shelving to hold her purses and shoes, a massive number of drawers, a full-length vanity, and inset dressing mirrors. Oh, and an elaborate crystal chandelier hanging in the center of the room to give the space even more glitz and glamour.

Natalie called it her dream closet, and Hailey had concurred while clearly expressing some serious closet envy. Wes, however, being a guy and an idiot, had grumbled about the unnecessary size and couldn't understand why she needed so many shoes and purses and clothes. Natalie had argued that size *did* matter and reminded Wes that she'd already more than compensated him for giving up one of the rooms in the house to make her happy. The smirk on Wes's face told everyone that said compensation had been in sexual favors, and Connor, Natalie's brother, immediately walked out of the room after announcing that he wasn't about to listen to the specifics of how Wes had exploited his baby sister.

"I think you got the better end of the deal," Kyle said to Wes as he leaned back in his chair and took a drink of his beer. "That man cave of yours down in the basement is fucking sweet and double the size of the one in your old house."

"Yeah, big enough for a theater room, a pool table, a poker table, and a full-service bar." Wes looked extremely pleased with himself. "Claiming the entire basement was part of my agreement with Natalie, along with an entire week of anytime/anywhere-I-want-them blow jobs," he said, just as Natalie and Hailey strolled out of the kitchen, each of them holding a bottle of Mike's Hard Lemonade.

"I still have rug burn on my knees because Wes wanted to make sure he got his week's worth," Natalie joked, a brazen contrast to the shyer, more modest Hailey walking beside her. "Trust me, I *earned* that closet."

"Jesus Christ," Connor said, shifting uncomfortably in his seat. "Will you two *stop?* I don't want to know or hear this shit about my sister."

Everyone laughed at the pained look on Connor's face, while Natalie slid into the seat next to Wes. Max watched Hailey walk around the table toward the vacant chair beside his, her blonde hair a soft, wavy cloud of silk that literally made his fingers itch to touch . . . and pull. She'd worn black jeans with heels and a pink off-the-shoulders blouse with a neckline trimmed in lace—the same color and fabric choice that she'd used to describe her panties to him yesterday afternoon. He wondered if she'd worn that particular top to deliberately tease him, and if so, it was definitely working.

When he'd first arrived with Hailey, they'd endured a bunch of ribbing from everyone about their fake engagement—Max wouldn't have expected anything less with this group—but once everyone had their fill of jokes and comments, Hailey had settled in nicely. She and Natalie seemed to hit it off well, and as Hailey settled into the seat beside his, she looked relaxed and comfortable.

"So, Hailey, this whole matchmaking thing you do, how does it work?" Kyle asked curiously.

"Why? Are you getting desperate for a date?" Wes interjected, trying to be funny.

"Ha-ha." Kyle gave Wes the middle finger. "No, wiseass. I have no problem finding women to date, and the last thing I'm looking for is to get serious with anyone." He shrugged. "I was just wondering how Hailey matches people."

"I'd like to know, too," Natalie said. "The whole matchmaking thing fascinates me. How did you even get into that kind of business?"

Hailey smiled, that self-consciousness coming into play again now that all the attention was on her. She was sitting close enough to him that he placed his hand on her thigh and gave it an encouraging squeeze.

"When I was in high school and through college, I had a knack for setting up my friends with guys who they really clicked with," she said easily. "When I graduated from college and I was unsure what I wanted to do, my best friend, Brielle, suggested I give professional matchmaking a try. So, I did."

"And you're obviously very successful at it," Natalie said, the words a compliment. "How does it all work?"

"It's very much like a dating site, but more personalized and upscale," she explained. "We personally meet and get to know all our clients, and they go through an extensive interview process so we can evaluate strengths, weaknesses, and what they're really looking for in a partner. From there, we have mixers and events, where a client can meet more than one person who fits their relationship criteria."

Natalie took a drink of her beverage before asking another question. "Do you do those compatibility tests? And do they really work?"

"Yes, they actually do," Hailey replied. "That gives us a lot of great information about a client's personality, so we can better match them to someone who has similar values and beliefs and interests."

Wes slid a hand across Natalie's shoulders and pulled her close, his lips tipping up in a humorous smile. "God, the two of us *never* would have gotten matched based on a compatibility test. She's a smartass and stubborn and competitive."

"Hey, that sounds just like you, Wes!" Kyle said, and rolled his eyes. "You two were made for each other. I don't think any other woman would put up with your crap the way Natalie does."

Natalie gave Kyle a sweet smile. "Thank you, Kyle."

The doorbell rang, and Natalie jumped up from her seat to answer the door. After a short conversation with the person on the front porch, the door closed and Natalie started toward the kitchen with three large boxes in her hands. "Pizza's here! Come and get it, boys."

Connor groaned and glared at Wes. "Are you fucking kidding me? Did you actually let Natalie order the pizzas after the last fiasco we had with her?"

"Yeah, we're getting married," Wes said, his expression sheepish. "Gotta start trusting her with the pizza order sometime."

Connor braced his hands on the table and pushed up to a standing position. "I'm going to wring her neck if there is so much as the scent of anchovies or jalapenos coming off of those pizzas. It took me *weeks* to be able to enjoy pizza again."

"You and me both, man," Kyle said, visibly shuddering as he followed Connor and Wes into the kitchen.

Max chuckled, vividly remembering that gawd-awful incident, and Hailey glanced at him with wide, curious eyes, prompting him to explain. "A few months ago, Natalie lost a bet to Wes, and he made her host one of our poker nights."

Natalie walked out of the kitchen with two slices of pizza on a plate, just in time to hear Max's comment. "In other words, Wes wanted me to be his maid so he could order me around and make me clean up their messes."

"Not true!" Wes shouted from the kitchen in his defense.

"Yeah, it's totally true," Max said, siding with Natalie because he knew Wes well enough to realize he'd been goading Natalie at the time. "So when he told her to order us some pizzas, they arrived with the most disgusting combinations. It was pretty gross. We all had to pick off the extra jalapenos and anchovies, and even then, it was pretty bad."

"No weird stuff tonight," Wes said as he heading into the dining room with his normal-looking pizza. "Promise." Then he sat down and leaned close to Natalie, nuzzling his face near her ear. "You did good, Minx," he murmured affectionately. "No spanking tonight, unless you want one, of course."

"Jesus Christ," Connor grumbled as he took his seat with his dinner. "I don't want to fucking know what goes on between you two. Seriously. It's creeping me out."

"Don't worry, Connor," Natalie said, not so innocently. "I wanted the spanking."

Connor swore again, and Hailey laughed at their bantering.

"Now that we know that the coast is clear, how about we go and get some pizza?" Max asked her.

Hailey smiled at him, her eyes bright with enjoyment. "That sounds good."

He scooted back his chair and stood and helped her up, too. Grabbing her hand in his, he led her into the kitchen. Kyle passed them on his way to the dining table with his own plate piled with pizza, which left the two of them alone for a few minutes.

Max handed her a plate, and he watched as she selected two slices from the box with pepperoni and mushroom. "Are you having a good time?"

"Yes, I am," she said, her voice light and happy. "I like your friends and Natalie is great, too."

He selected three slices of the meat lovers' combo. "I'm glad you like them. They can be a bit crazy sometimes, as you can see, but it's all in good fun."

They carried their plates back to the table and joined his friends, joking and laughing and telling stories as they ate their dinner. Hailey helped Natalie with the cleanup, and they stayed for another hour after that until Max announced they were going to head out. The next day, Monday, was an early work day for all of them, and while Max had enjoyed the evening with his friends, he wanted some alone time with Hailey before he went home, too.

Half an hour later, Max parked his car outside of Hailey's apartment building and walked her to her door, then followed her inside once it was unlocked and open. He closed it behind them, and because he'd been dying to get his hands and mouth on her all night, he took her keys and purse from her hands, set them on a side table, and buried his hands in her hair.

He guided her a few steps back, until she was pressed up against the nearest wall. A soft gasp escaped her, and her eyes warmed with instantaneous longing. Having her against a hard surface was a familiar position for the two of them, and it enabled him to align his entire body along the length of hers, as well as maintain control of the situation. And standing, instead of reclining on a comfortable couch, also kept him from taking things too far, too fast with her tonight.

He tipped her head up, positioning her mouth right where he wanted it, just inches below his. Her lips parted on a soft sigh, and he smiled. "It's only been three days since I've kissed you, but it feels like forever."

"I agree," she whispered as she slid her hands between the two of them and up to his chest. "You were too much of a gentleman when you picked me up earlier. I wanted you to kiss me then."

Ahhh, he liked the fact that her anticipation was growing, that she was becoming less guarded with him, as well as embracing her desires rather than trying to hide or suppress them. He supposed a lot of it had to do with their intimate phone conversations and texts, which were gradually breaking down those insecurities and giving her the confidence to be more open and adventurous. Once the mind was swayed and seduced, he was hopeful her body would follow.

He gently skimmed the pads of his thumbs along her soft cheeks. "I guess I'll have to make up for that kiss now, won't I?"

"Yes, I think so, too," she said eagerly.

Her lashes fluttered closed in the sweetest kind of surrender, her upturned lips waiting for him to claim them, and he wasn't about to disappoint her. His lips covered hers, and she immediately responded to the firm pressure with a sensual moan. She welcomed the soft sweep of his tongue inside her mouth and shuddered against him as he stroked and teased and coaxed her to play along.

Her body rubbed uninhibitedly against his, her hips gyrating in a way that drove him insane with wanting her. His dick was hard and aching, and when she made a needy sound in the back of her throat, he tipped her head back farther and delved more deeply, more greedily, so hungry for her that it took every ounce of control he possessed to rein it all back in while he could still think straight.

With effort, he ended the kiss and buried his face against the side of her neck with a low, growling groan, very much aware of her chest heaving against his and the luscious swells of her breasts tempting him. Considering the off-the-shoulder blouse she was wearing, he could have easily tugged down her top to bare those gorgeous tits to his gaze and suck on those tight, aroused nipples he could feel demanding his attention between them. Any other woman, and he probably would have.

They already had the kissing and touching down to a fine art, and in that regard, they were completely in sync. But that next step between them was huge, and he didn't want to fuck it up by rushing things with Hailey and scaring her off. She was getting there at her own pace, trusting him more and more, and he was patient enough to wait.

He lifted his head and stared down at blue eyes blurred with desire and her lips damp and swollen from his kiss. "I need to go," he said, his tone gruff with the effort to resist her.

Her teeth grazed that lush lower lip, her expression demure. "Are you sure you don't want to stay?"

He knew what that invitation was insinuating, and it wasn't a request to stay for a glass of ice tea and conversation. She was definitely getting more comfortable with him physically, but right now, he had a feeling that the adrenaline rush of arousal thrumming through her body was overriding her normal uncertainties, and he wasn't about to take advantage of her offer when he knew she wasn't mentally prepared for that next level of intimacy. The last thing he wanted was for her to have regrets after the fact.

"Not tonight," he said with a shake of his head.

Confusion swirled in her gaze. "Why not?"

God, she was killing him with those big blue eyes. "Believe me when I say that, more than anything, I want to stay right here with you, but there's two reasons I can't," he said, knowing he was doing the right thing, even if his dick was currently protesting. "For one thing, we haven't negotiated that part of our relationship yet, and secondly and more importantly, you're not quite ready to beg. But we're definitely getting there."

Much to his relief, she didn't take it as a rejection. Instead, a flirty smile eased up the corners of her mouth. "Then I think you need to step up your game."

He laughed. "Challenge accepted."

Chapter Eight

HAILEY GLANCED AT her reflection in the full-length mirror attached to the inside of her closet door, giving her outfit one more inspection. She'd spent the past two hours trying to find something appropriate to wear to Max's father's birthday barbeque, and she was pretty certain she'd finally found *the* dress. She'd gone through dozens of choices, and while she kept muttering to herself that she had nothing to wear, the huge pile of clothes on the bed contradicted that statement.

Today, it was all about looking the part of Max's fiancée to meet his family, and considering how much she'd fretted over what to wear, she would have thought that the engagement was real and legitimate. It wasn't, of course. She was accompanying Max today to hopefully stop his mother from her meddling attempts and to put an end to Addison thinking she had some kind of chance with Max. But knowing all that didn't stop Hailey from wanting to fit in and hoping that his family liked her.

The fitting in part concerned her the most. While a lot of her clients were wealthy and affluent, she hadn't grown up in the lap of luxury as Max had. In fact, she still tried to live modestly, and her biggest fear was sticking out like a sore thumb and being judged, even if Max had reassured her that she wouldn't be.

"I think this is it," she said to her reflection as she smoothed a hand down the front of the knee-length dress. The fabric was a pretty spring pattern that was modest and casual and perfect for an outdoor party in the afternoon. The cut of the dress was super-flattering, with a rounded neckline that didn't overly expose her breasts. The design nipped in at the waist and flared out at the hips to minimize her extra curves—which was a good thing since she was bravely forgoing her Spanx today.

Nerves and anticipation fluttered in her stomach, and those butterflies weren't just over meeting his parents. Nearly a week had passed since the night he'd kissed her goodnight after their evening at Wes and Natalie's and her playful comment for Max to step up his game, and he hadn't missed an opportunity to do exactly that.

Between both of their work schedules and Hailey packing up her house and office for the move in her spare time, they'd managed to find time to spend together. They'd gone to lunch twice—once after he'd accompanied her to the property inspection for the Logan Square building and again after she'd dropped paperwork off to her lender—and both times had ended with a hot kiss that made her melt. Throughout the day, random messages would appear on her phone, bold, sexy texts that made her blush and always required an answer from her: What is the most sensitive part of your body? *My neck.* Give a massage or get a massage? *Give a massage.* Would she rather have sex in the shower or a tub? *Tub full of bubbles.* Lights on or lights dimmed? *Lights dimmed.* And at least a dozen more questions.

At night, they talked on the phone, about work, their childhoods, and he gave her a rundown of his family for today's party, but those calls always ended the same way . . . with a provocative question that coaxed her to open up to him sexually, and always left her aching and wanting him. Slowly and gradually, all week long, he'd chipped away at her doubts and insecurities, and last night, after a heavy-duty session of phone sex, when she was quivering in the aftermath of another intense orgasm, he'd asked the one question that would change everything between them.

Are you ready to beg, sweet girl?

Her answer had come without hesitation, because she trusted him. *Yes.*

And his husky, seductive reply . . . *Tomorrow evening, after the party, I promise you will.*

So, yes, tonight was *the* night. She was nervous, but she was also ready, mentally and physically. She'd never wanted another man as much as she wanted Max, and she'd be stupid to pass up the opportunity to have a passionate affair with him. Who knew when it would happen again? Once their fake engagement was over, and the end was certainly inevitable, it was most likely back to her battery-operated boyfriend for the foreseeable future. But at least she'd have plenty of fantasies of Max stored up to keep her warm at night.

Refusing to think about the end of their ar-

rangement before it even happened, she finished getting ready, distracting herself by trying
on some shoes before settling on a pair of white
strappy sandals with a three-inch heel. After
adding a few silver bangle bracelets to her wrist
and a pair of earrings in her lobes, she removed
the hot rollers from her hair and combed her
fingers through the waves so they cascaded
down her back, then touched up her makeup
and spritzed on her favorite perfume.

That didn't leave her much time to
overthink things, since she finished her primp-
ing at five minutes to four, and minutes later
there was a knock on the door. Knowing it was
Max, she rushed to answer, her heart beating a
little faster when she laid eyes on him, struck, as
always, by what a devastatingly gorgeous man
he was. She'd thought she'd get used to just
how sexy he was by now, but each time she saw
him, the breathless, giddy feeling only seemed
to increase.

His hair was its normal tousled style, and he
was wearing a casual, light blue collared shirt, a
pair of tan pants that displayed his lean hips and
toned thighs, and a pair of leather loafers. His
hands were in his pockets, and the slow, ap-
praising smile on his face as he looked her over

from head to toe, then back again, made her weak in the knees.

"Do you want to come in?" she managed to ask politely. "I just need to grab my purse and I'm ready to go."

He shook his head. "I'm not stepping inside of your apartment, because if I do, we'll never leave. Okay, that's a lie. We'll leave *eventually*, and you'll look completely disheveled and we'll be making a fashionably late entrance."

Being late was the last thing she wanted, even if his idea tempted her. "I'm trying to impress your family, not have them think I'm some diva who can't get ready on time."

He leaned against the doorjamb, grinning. "Or they'll take one look at your pretty face, flushed from an orgasm or two, and just think that I can't keep my hands off you."

Her bad, bad nipples furled tight at the erotic images he'd just inserted into her mind. "I thought that was tonight."

"Exactly," he said, wicked humor dancing in his eyes. "Which is why I'm staying put right where I am, with my hands in my pockets. So hurry and get your purse before I change my mind."

She was pretty sure he was just teasing her,

but not wanting to take any chances, she didn't waste time getting her handbag and meeting him back in the entryway. She closed and locked the door, and he grabbed her hand and walked with her to his vehicle, a black Range Rover that was rugged on the outside and luxurious and roomy on the inside.

Once they were on I-90 West heading toward South Barrington, Hailey glanced at Max, thinking back to a few days ago when he'd told her that he'd finally dropped the news of their engagement on his mother and father, to give them some time to absorb the announcement before Max brought her to the party to meet everyone.

"So, are your parents over the shock of your quick, spontaneous engagement to me?" she asked, trying to sound upbeat about it all when she really had no idea what to expect when they arrived.

"Actually, my mom called me this morning," he said, casting a smile her way. "She's anxious to meet you."

"I'll bet she is," she said wryly.

He laughed, the sound light and humorous. "Let me rephrase that. She's *excited* to meet you."

She rolled her eyes. "You don't have to lie."

"I'm not. I swear." Another quick look in Hailey's direction revealed his serious expression. "What you fail to understand is that my mother *wants* me to get married. Badly. That's why she pushed Addison on me, and a half a dozen women before her. She's the kind of mother who doesn't think any of her children can truly be happy without having a wife or, in my sister's case, a husband, and a house in the suburbs and kids. She's a hopeless romantic, and if she and my father eloped after three months and have been married for nearly forty years, then this is not a farfetched concept for her to believe that we're in love in such a short time, too."

Hailey wanted to ask, *what if your mother doesn't like me?* But in the scheme of things, did that really matter? No, because this wasn't a real engagement. It was a temporary arrangement and all for show, for both of them.

"Don't get me wrong," Max continued on. "I'm sure my mother will ask you a ton of questions, but I swear it's not an interrogation. She's genuinely curious about you."

She appreciated the warning. As Max navigated the road, Hailey thought about everything he'd told her about his family during their many conversations this past week, just to make sure that all the facts were fresh in her mind. He was the youngest of three siblings, and both his brother and sister were married with kids, and his sister was pregnant with her third child. Both Max's brother and his sister's husband worked at his father's law firm, and she smiled when she remembered how he'd called himself the black sheep of the family since he was the only son in many generations who hadn't become a lawyer. Legalese was so not Max's thing, but he loved real estate, and that's where his true passion lay.

The fact that his parents had supported his decision told Hailey how much they cared about Max. His happiness was what mattered to them, and there was no disappointment over the fact that he hadn't followed in a family tradition that he had no interest in. They sounded like good people, and a part of her felt a twinge of guilt that they were about to deceive his family.

Then there was Addison, another component to today's visit. "Where do things stand between you and Addison?" she asked Max, because she wanted to be prepared. As much as possible, she wanted to know what to expect from the other woman. "Did your mom tell Addison's mother the news about us?" And from there, Hailey had no doubt the information would trickle down to the daughter.

"Yes. My mother said Addison's mother was devastated over the news, which sounds a bit dramatic to me," he said, taking his eyes off the road for a moment to flash her a sardonic smile. "Addison has texted me a few times, wanting to know how I could move on so quickly and asking questions about you. How we met, how long we've been dating, that sort of thing."

The fact that Addison had grilled Max about her made Hailey's stomach uneasy. From everything Max had told her, the other woman was persistent and insistent. She clearly wanted Max, so how far would she go to try and keep him even if he'd made it clear he wasn't interested?

"And what did you say to her?" Hailey asked.

"The same thing I've been telling her all along," he said with a shrug. "For weeks, even before you and I started dating, I texted her at least a dozen times that I was seeing someone, and yeah, at first it was a lie to get her to back off, but it works for our timeline. I told her we met through work, which is what my parents think, too. As for telling her about you, well, I didn't give her any information, because, quite frankly, it's none of her damn business."

Hailey bit back a smile, grateful that Max hadn't caved to Addison's demands. Then again, she got the distinct impression that he didn't do *anything* he didn't want to.

After a forty-minute drive, they arrived in South Barrington, an upscale neighborhood with luxurious custom-built homes that were separated by acres of land in between. Max pulled into a long, paved driveway that led up to a sprawling house with a gray stone facade and a few other high-end vehicles parked near the four-car garage. She stared in awe at the estate home, taking in the lush, immaculate landscaping and the gorgeous marble water fountain out front that had to have cost a small fortune.

"Wow, the house is beautiful . . . and huge," she said, speaking her thoughts out loud.

"I agree." He chuckled as he turned off the car and removed the keys from the ignition. "It's way too much house for my parents, but my mother, being the sentimental person she is, refuses to move even though my father has suggested it more than once. My parents bought the house when we kids were really young, and she says there are too many memories for her to give up the place. All of our rooms are like time capsules back to when we were in high school, and she insists on keeping them that way so *our* kids can sleep in each of our rooms when they stay over."

He glanced at her with a warm smile. "My mother keeps telling me that *my* room is getting full of cobwebs because it's the only one not being used. Total guilt trip."

She laughed. "I already like your mom."

"Are you ready to head inside?" he asked. "We're a little early, per my mother's request so I have time to introduce you to the family before all the guests arrive."

Exhaling a deep, fortifying breath, she nodded. "I'm ready."

"Then let's do this," he said with a playful wink.

They both got out of the car, and she came around to his side. He automatically entwined his fingers with hers, then led the way along the walkway to the small porch. She knew he was probably holding her hand because it was a sweet and romantic gesture for his parents' benefit, but she liked the way it made her feel safe and protected, as well as calmed the nerves springing to life inside her again.

As soon as they reached the porch, he turned toward her with a smile so affectionate it made her heart trip in her chest. Then he reached up and gently brushed a stray strand of her hair away from her cheek, his touch both sensual and tender at the same time.

"By the way, I meant to tell you back at your apartment that you look absolutely stunning, and I wanted you to know that before we go inside," he said, skimming his thumb along her jaw. "Also, I know you're nervous, but trust me when I tell you that there's nothing about you that my family won't adore as much as I do."

Hearing compliments from a man was a rare occurrence for her, but hearing them from Max, a man she knew she was steadily falling for, made her wish that everything between them was real. "Thank you," she said softly.

The corner of his mouth quirked into a flirtatious smile as he dipped his head toward hers. "You're welcome," he murmured, and settled his lips on hers for a sweet kiss that lingered long enough to make her yearn for more.

The door suddenly opened, startling Hailey so badly she literally jumped away from Max. Realizing they'd just been caught in the act, her face heated as she looked at the older woman standing on the other side of the threshold. In her late fifties, she was slender and very pretty, with dark brown hair and the same hazel eyes as Max. Her smile was so filled with an undeniable excitement that it was nearly infectious.

"I'm so sorry to interrupt you two," she said on a rush of breath as she clasped her hands to her chest, her kind gaze taking in everything about Hailey. "I saw the two of you drive up, and I just couldn't wait any longer to meet my soon-to-be daughter-in-law!"

Max chuckled. "Way to ruin a romantic moment, Mom,"

"Oh, hush, Maximilian," she said, waving her hand at Max in a chastising manner. "You've kept this treasure a secret and have had her all to yourself for long enough. It's time to share her with the rest of the family."

Max glanced at Hailey with an unmistakable *I told you so* look on his face.

His mother unexpectedly reached out and caught Hailey's face between her soft palms and looked her in the eyes, her expression sincere.

"You are just as beautiful as Max said you were, not that I had any doubts whatsoever. Now come inside so you can meet everyone else before the party gets started."

Before Hailey could say anything at all, his mother hooked her arm through Hailey's and guided her into the massive foyer, decorated with marble flooring and boasting a grand double staircase that led to the second story of the house.

Trying not to get too overwhelmed by it all, Hailey managed a courteous smile. "It's a pleasure to meet you, Mrs. Sterling."

"Please, call me Grace," she insisted, patting Hailey's hand as she led her toward the back of the house.

Hailey glanced over her shoulder at Max, who was following them. He gave her a lopsided smile, clearly used to his mother's audacious personality, and mouthed the words, *just go with it.*

She didn't think she had any other option with Grace whisking her into a spacious, warmly decorated family room where a group of people and some young kids were hanging out.

"Hailey is here!" Grace announced happily,

and everyone went quiet as they all turned to stare at her.

A beautiful brunette who looked like Max was the first to approach her, a hand on her very pregnant belly and an amicable smile on her face, while two little rambunctious boys ran straight past Hailey shouting, "Uncle Max! You're here!"

The woman in front of her laughed as she gave Hailey a quick, warm hug. "I'm Max's sister, Kristen, and this is my husband, Michael," she said, introducing the good-looking man by her side.

She greeted both of them, followed by Max's brother, Alex, and his wife, Brittany, and finally, Mr. Sterling, who insisted on being called Douglas—all of whom hugged her, as well.

Kristen waved to the two boys now wrestling with Max on the rug. "And those two wild heathens belong to me. The bigger one is Tyler, and Morgan is the blond one," she said, giving Hailey a way to identify each boy.

Two little girls stood on each side of Alex's legs, peering at Hailey curiously with pretty green eyes, and their father was quick to introduce them, too. "And this here is Shelley, and her sister, Sara."

"It's very nice to meet you all," Hailey said, grateful that Max had briefed her on everyone, which made it so much easier to put a face with those names.

"Uncle Max!" Tyler said, pulling insistently on Max's hand. "Will you come outside and throw the football for us like you always do?"

Max glanced at her, silently asking Hailey if she'd be okay without him for a while, and she smiled in return. "Go have fun with your nephews."

"Yippee!" the two boys cheered, and ran out of the room.

Max came up to her, a subtle but unmistakable wicked glimmer in his eyes, and right in front of everyone, he kissed her on the cheek, causing her to blush, as usual. "I'll see you in a little bit, sweetheart."

Oh, yeah, he was totally pouring on the charm, and by the delighted looks on his sister's and mother's faces, they were definitely fooled into believing that Max was head over heels for her.

Grace shooed the rest of the men out of the room. "How about *all* you boys head outside and get yourself a beer or drink before the guests start arriving, and us girls will check on things in the kitchen."

With that suggestion, the men dispersed, and Hailey followed Kristen and Grace into the gourmet kitchen. The space was painted white, with stainless steel state-of-the-art appliances and a huge island in the center of the room topped with a quartz countertop. Hailey quickly realized that there wasn't much to check on, considering a barbeque was about to happen and no one else was in the kitchen. But a glance out the window over the sink revealed a spacious outdoor area being set up by caterers and casually dressed waiters who were in charge of preparing all the food for the party. Next to that was a full-service bar with a hired bartender, where the men were already gathered and placing their orders.

"Have a seat, Hailey," Grace said, indicating the row of stools tucked under the center island. "What can I get you to drink? A glass of wine or champagne? Or a cocktail? We also have lemonade and sweet tea."

Hailey definitely wanted to keep her wits about her today, mostly because she was anticipating a meeting with Addison at some point. "I'd love a glass of lemonade. Thank you."

"I'll have the same, Mom," Kristen said, taking a seat beside Hailey with a soft groan and a hand on her stomach.

"When are you due?" Hailey asked her while Grace poured the drinks.

"I've got six more weeks to go." Kristen released a tired sigh. "This little girl's birthday cannot come soon enough."

"A girl," Hailey said, happy for the other woman since she already had two boys. "How wonderful."

"Actually, I would have stopped at two boys, but Michael really wanted a girl. I gave him one more try, and he managed to get it right this time." Kristen laughed.

"The more grandbabies there are, the happier I am," Grace said merrily as she set a glass of lemonade in front Hailey and Kristen, then took a spot across from them on the other side of the island. "How many children do you and Max plan on having?"

"Mom!" Kristen admonished, and shook her head. "Hailey *just* met us."

"What?" Grace batted her eyes innocently at her daughter. "They're engaged. I'm sure they've discussed having a family."

Hailey took a drink of the sweetened lemonade to give herself a moment to think. The last thing she wanted to do was outright fib to Max's mother, which was ridiculous since they were perpetuating an enormous lie—and neither did she want to get the other woman's hopes up since their arrangement was temporary.

"Max and I both want a family, when the time is right," she replied, keeping things as vague as possible yet reassuring Grace at the same time. "But right now, I'm focused on my business, so it might be a little while."

"A matchmaking agency, right?" Kristen asked, her expression reflecting her interest. "How does all that work?"

The subject was an easy one for Hailey to talk about, and she answered every question that Kristen asked, and there were plenty. Her career was an endless source of fascination to a lot of people, and Hailey was used to their curiosity.

Kristen took a moment to sip her lemonade, and Grace took that as her opportunity to jump into the conversation, asking Hailey where she'd grown up and about her family. She told them everything that Max knew about her past, her parents' deaths, and being raised by her aunt and uncle. She knew they were curious about her—and had every right to be considering they believed she was marrying Max. It wasn't quite an interrogation, and neither did they ask their questions with suspicion, but she definitely felt as though she was in the hot seat.

"Max mentioned that he's helping out at an upcoming charity event for Mercy Home for Boys & Girls," Grace said. "A carnival, I believe, yes?"

Hailey nodded. "I've been involved with the charity for the past year or so through the agency and roped Max into helping, too. It's next weekend, and I'm not sure which booth I'll be working at, but if you're free, it would be great to have you stop by and support the charity." She glanced at Kristen. "And there's plenty for the boys to do, too. Rides, games, food, and more."

Kristen smiled. "That sounds like a fun day."

"There are a group of us ladies who are always looking for a good cause to support," Grace said from across the counter. "I'll let them know about it, as well. Are donations accepted, too?"

"Absolutely."

"Then I'll make sure I bring a check with me."

An unexpected donation would make Maureen happy, Hailey knew.

"So, I'm dying to know . . . have you and Max talked about a wedding date?" Grace asked unabashedly. "His father and I got married three months after we first met."

Hailey inhaled a deep breath as she settled her hands in her lap and absently twisted the ring on her finger to stave off her anxiety. It was so much easier to talk about her matchmaking business, and even her family situation, instead of addressing the future with Max. Hailey smiled at Grace as her reply came to mind.

"No date set yet," she answered honestly. "Everything has happened so fast between Max and me, and now that we're engaged, we just want to slow down and enjoy each other for a while."

"Well, you can certainly do that while being married, too," Grace suggested oh-so-helpfully.

"Mom, give poor Hailey a break," Kristen said, exasperated. "It'll happen when they're ready. Just be happy that Max is finally getting married. We all thought he'd be a bachelor for the rest of his life."

Kristen's comment was laced with amusement, but Hailey realized that what she'd just disclosed matched exactly what Max had said to her the day they'd had lunch together, when he'd told her about Addison. *What my mother doesn't understand, no matter how many times I've tried to tell her, is that I'm perfectly content with my life and being a bachelor.*

She'd known that about Max. While this fake engagement was fun and flirty for the time that they were together, and he was great at playing the loving fiancé in front of his family and when it mattered, his sister's remark solidified what Hailey already knew—that no matter what happened between them over the next few weeks, Max would never *really* be hers. Bachelor comment aside, did she really have what it took to keep a man like Max interested beyond a fun, flirty affair?

The pit in her stomach also revealed that she'd secretly been harboring hope things between them might . . . last. Thank goodness his sister had set her straight on that account, reminding her exactly where things stood between her and Max. No more lying to herself, even if she hadn't realized she'd been doing it.

"I never believed Max would be a bachelor for the rest of his life," Grace said, contradicting Kristen's statement. "I know *he* said it, but I also knew it was just a matter of him finding the right girl to change his mind."

Hailey hated the uneasy sensation settling over her. She was also starting to feel a bit antsy and in need of fresh air but wasn't sure how to gracefully excuse herself from the conversation. She certainly didn't want to be rude or offend Grace or Kristen, but stepping outdoors and being in a wide-open space instead of feeling confined in the kitchen was starting to sound really good at the moment.

As if Max had telepathic powers and knew she'd reached her limit for now and needed a break, he walked into the kitchen, triggering a sense of relief in Hailey.

"Guests are starting to arrive, ladies," he announced. He came up to Hailey and slid a hand up her back and beneath her hair in an intimate caress, until his fingers were touching the nape of her neck. "You've had your time with Hailey, and now I'm here to steal away my fiancée."

Grace beamed at her son. "I can't tell you

how happy I am for the two of you."

"I know, Mom," he said, his tone wry. Folding Hailey's hand in his, he brought the backs of her fingers to his lips. "We're happy, too."

Oh, boy, was he pouring it on thick. As Max stared into her eyes in the pretense of being a love-struck fool, she was certain he could see the amusement glimmering in the depths of her gaze, and his own mouth quirked in an equally playful smile.

Keeping her close to his side, he escorted her outside at the back of the house, which was just as astounding as everything else on this property. The patio was enormous, with tables and chairs set up for dozens of guests and an area to use as a dance floor if anyone wanted to take advantage of the music the DJ was playing. Off to the side was a fire pit, and down a pathway was a pool with a waterfall.

As people started arriving, Max shook hands with family friends and introduced her, as well. While everyone was nice and amicable, Hailey couldn't deny that she felt a bit out of place. There was no refuting the guests were all wealthy based on their designer clothing, the jewelry they wore, and that certain air about them that just spoke of upper class. Max's mom also proudly announced Hailey as Max's fiancée, and she did her best to accept everyone's congratulations with poise and grace.

As Max drew her away from an older couple they'd just met and Hailey thought she'd finally have a moment to breathe without the pressure of being the center of attention, he gave her hand a squeeze and bent his head so his mouth was closer to her ear and no one else could hear what he had to say.

"I know you're probably tired of meeting new people, and I hate to do this to you, but Addison and her parents are right over there, and we might as well get the greetings over with."

She nodded in understanding, and sliding her hand into the crook of his arm, she let Max lead her toward Addison and her parents. The gorgeous young woman was already eyeing Hailey critically. . . and no doubt finding her lacking in comparison to herself. Truth be told, Addison was everything that Hailey wasn't— slender, refined, and sophisticated. The other woman was certainly intimidating, and most of all, Addison fit in with this wealthy crowd like the socialite she was.

Hailey's stupid insecurities tried to claw

their way to the surface, and she reminded herself that Max had never, ever made her feel less than beautiful, and *she* was the one currently on his arm, not Addison. And it was that thought that gave her the fortitude to put on a smile and greet the other woman with decorum and confidence.

Chapter Nine

"**M**AX, IT'S NICE to see you." Addison's mother, Priscilla Brooks was the first to greet him, the pleasant tone of her voice contradicting the judgmental look on her face.

Like mother, like daughter, Max thought, but refused to give either of them the satisfaction of making this any more awkward for himself or Hailey.

"It's nice to see you as well, Mr. and Mrs. Brooks and Addison," he said, addressing the trio like the polite gentleman his mother had raised him to be, no matter the circumstance. "This is my fiancée, Hailey Ellison."

"It's a pleasure to meet you," Hailey said graciously, and offered her hand to Priscilla, then Addison, both of whom tentatively responded with a limp, weak handshake, as if being forced to touch something distasteful.

A tight, fake smile pulled up the corners of Priscilla's lips. "I truly thought your mother was joking when she told me that you'd gotten engaged," she said, the underlying censure in her voice coming through loud and clear. "It was only a short while ago that you were in a relationship with Addison."

Oh, yeah, shots were being fired. He'd gone out with Addison a total of *three* times, two of which had been forced upon him by his good-intentioned mother. Hardly a relationship by Max's standards, but he wasn't about to argue the point. Neither was he about to call out Addison for her stalker-ish behavior over the past five weeks or the passive-aggressive texts she'd sent him in her attempts to change his mind about her. Priscilla was friendly with his mother, and her husband was one of Max's father's biggest clients. There was no way he was going to say or do anything that reflected badly on him. It just wasn't his style.

Before he could reply to Priscilla's comment, Mr. Brooks cleared his throat, seemingly uncomfortable with his wife's dig, as well. "I think I'm going to head to the bar for a drink.

Care to join me, Max?"

He felt Hailey stiffen beside him at the thought of being left alone with these two women, which wasn't something Max would ever deliberately do. Ever so gently, he skimmed his thumb over the back of the hand still holding on to his arm in a calm, soothing gesture and shook his head at Mr. Brooks. "No, thank you, sir. I'm good."

Priscilla's husband was quick to take his leave, and for some reason, with him gone, the tension between the four of them grew thicker. Max was just about to excuse himself and Hailey, but before he could say anything, Addison spoke.

"I have to say, Max, from what I've heard, I thought you had a *type*," Addison said, as if Hailey weren't even there. "You definitely surprised us with your new fiancée. She's not quite what we . . . expected."

Max clenched his jaw. Addison's words weren't a direct insult, but he knew that had been her intention, and he found her comment offensive. No, Hailey didn't look like the slender women he usually dated, but then again, he'd never deliberately dated a woman solely based on her size. He fucking hated that Addison was shallow enough to judge Hailey without knowing her and find gratification in tearing down another woman's self-esteem.

Any other time, any other place, and he would have had some choice words of his own to say to Addison. But his father's sixtieth birthday party, around a few dozen influential guests, was not the place to engage in a confrontation. He couldn't imagine what his mother had seen in Addison to believe that she'd be someone he'd ever be interested in. On the other hand, his kindhearted mother was the type to believe the best of everyone, and obviously somewhere along the way, Addison had portrayed herself much differently than the woman standing in front of him now.

"Actually, Addison, just so we're clear, I never really had a *type*," he said, addressing her rude remark in the politest way possible. "But Hailey is, hands down, everything I could ever want in a woman and a fiancée, so I have to consider myself damn lucky that I met her." Which was Max's way of letting Addison know she hadn't been the right female for him. Just as he'd been trying to tell her for the last who knew how long.

The spiteful look in Addison's eyes as she

looked from Hailey to him made his blood boil. And Priscilla was just as bad as she looked down her nose at Hailey just as disdainfully. He wasn't about to spend another minute subjecting one of the kindest, sweetest women he knew to this bitch and her snooty mother.

He exhaled a calming breath and kept his tone neutral. "I hope you both enjoy your evening," he said, and led Hailey far away from the duo.

"Jesus Christ, I need a drink," he muttered irritably. He headed for the bar as he glanced at Hailey, unable to imagine how difficult that encounter had been for her. "I'm so sorry about that. About them. Are you all right?"

"Max, I'm fine. Really," she assured him with a brittle smile that told him she'd been affected by the hurtful things Addison had said. "You warned me what she was like, and I've dealt with plenty of judgmental people. Hopefully, after today you won't have to put up with her any longer. Let's just try and enjoy your father's party, okay?"

God, he felt like shit. And here she was, thoughtful and caring about his parents' party. After what had just happened, after she'd been a direct target of Addison's and her mother's nasty comments, she was more concerned about him than herself.

Abruptly, he stopped walking, and not giving a damn who was watching, he brought his hands up to Hailey's face. Her eyes grew wide in startled surprise, and he didn't hesitate to touch his lips to hers in a soft, lingering kiss. An affectionate yet intimate kiss that hopefully told her how rare and special she was. He felt her sigh against his mouth, felt her body relax as she tentatively placed her own hands on his waist.

"Ahhh, to be young and in love," he heard his mother say dreamily from somewhere nearby, which made Max grin against Hailey's mouth before he lifted his head and ended the kiss.

"Yes, it's awesome to be in love," he said in response to his mother's comment, playing the part of devoted fiancé.

But as he said the words and stared into Hailey's warm blue eyes, his heart felt as though it had expanded in his chest. No, he wasn't in love with Hailey, but he knew without a doubt he was quickly heading in that direction, and he was oddly okay with that because it felt right. She felt right.

"There's someone I want Hailey to meet,"

Grace said, interrupting the thoughts in Max's head. For now, anyway, because that realization he'd just come to was definitely worth revisiting later.

Grace led them to an older couple. The man was one of Max's father's oldest friends. Introductions were made, along with congratulations on their engagement. From there, the next few hours passed quickly as he and Hailey mingled with friends and family, though it irritated the hell out of Max the numerous times he'd caught Addison watching them from a distance. A bit too obsessively if you asked him. He knew that Hailey had seen her watching, too, which made him feel even more protective of her—and determined not to give Addison any opportunity to be alone with Hailey at any point of the evening.

A delicious barbeque dinner was served buffet-style with ribs and chicken and an assortment of side dishes. While he'd piled his plate high, he noticed that Hailey was more moderate in her selections, which he understood better now that she'd explained her struggle with her weight. Considering her childhood, he could only guess that she had a love-hate relationship with food and tried to be conscious about what she ate, but he never wanted her to feel like a number on a scale mattered to him. She was healthy and curvy and sexy as hell, and he liked her just the way she was.

The afternoon turned to dusk, and as the sun went down, the twinkling lights stringing across the lattice patio came on. The guests enjoyed the great playlist of music the DJ had put together, and Max even managed to coax Hailey out on the dance floor a few times, enjoying the way she smiled and laughed as he and his brother entertained everyone with a break-dance routine they'd choreographed when they were teenagers and shockingly still remembered.

When that was over and the next fast-paced song began, Max's father grabbed Hailey's hand, spun her around, and proceeded to dance with her—giving Hailey his stamp of approval in his own quiet, unique way. And again, Addison watched them from the sidelines, drinking glass after glass of champagne and looking more and more jealous and resentful as the night went on.

The two-tiered birthday cake was brought out and placed at a dessert table that was already overflowing with an array of cookies, candies, tarts, and a tray of sliced fruits to dip into the chocolate fountain. His father blew out the six and zero candles on top of the cake, and the caterers began slicing and plating the dessert for everyone.

"Let's go get a piece of cake," Max said as he led Hailey off the dance floor, loving the effervescent sparkle in her eyes and the flush on her cheeks. "My mother told me it was red velvet with cream cheese filling, which is not only my dad's favorite but mine, too."

She grinned at him. "I think I burned enough extra calories to enjoy a slice of cake, and maybe even a few pieces of fruit dipped in chocolate."

Even if she hadn't, he wanted her to enjoy every aspect of the evening, and he would have insisted she indulge. They started toward the dessert table, but a family friend stopped Max on the way, wanting to talk real estate and the current market. He didn't want to be rude and brush the guy off, and he must have looked torn, because Hailey gave his hand a squeeze and said, "You two talk. I'll go grab a few pieces of cake and meet you back at our table."

He watched Hailey walk away, and while he answered all of Joe Kershaw's questions, Max managed to keep her in his line of sight. At the dessert table, his mother and sister stopped to talk to her, and she laughed at something they said before picking up two slices of cake, then moving over to the chocolate fountain, where she added a few pieces of drenched fruit on both of their plates.

As Joe went on about his interest in investment properties, Hailey headed toward the table where they'd eaten dinner, a happy smile on her face, until Addison stepped right in front of her, a little unsteady on her feet—most likely from too much alcohol—and brought Hailey to a sudden stop.

He couldn't see Addison's face, but as she spoke to Hailey, her entire body stiffened and her expression gradually changed—from cheerful to wary to pained. Hailey flinched, as though whatever words Addison had spoken were the equivalent to a physical blow, and every protective instinct Max possessed surged through him in an adrenaline rush of anger.

Max quickly excused himself from the discussion with Joe, telling the other man to give him a call at the office and they could talk more in depth about his interests in a more focused setting, then strode toward Hailey. Before he could reach the two women, Addison walked away, leaving Hailey standing there in shock, her complexion pale and her features reflecting her distress.

Fuck. He increased his stride, getting to her as quickly as he could, and when he was finally standing in front of her, he noticed that her hands were shaking and the forks on the plates were rattling. He took both dishes and gave them to a passing waitress to take care of, then took her hands in his to still their trembling.

"What the fuck did Addison say to you?" he demanded to know, his rage simmering right below the surface.

She shook her head, her eyes so filled with pain it made him want to punch his fist through something, just to release some of the fury boiling in his veins. "Nothing," she whispered, the raw tone of her voice sounding as if Addison had literally sucked the life out of her. "It was nothing."

"It wasn't *nothing*," he growled, trying to keep a tight rein on his temper. "Tell me what she said, Hailey."

She swallowed hard and glanced down at his chest, her reluctance palpable. "She said . . . I really ought to cut back on the cake and take better care of myself if I ever expect to keep a man like you . . . although she was certain that your interest in me wouldn't last long, anyway."

He swore out loud and jerked his head up, immediately searching for Addison. When he found her, he let go of Hailey's hands but only managed to take one step in the other woman's direction before Hailey grabbed his arm to stop him.

"Don't," she pleaded desperately. "They're just words, Max, and I'm fine. And she's not worth making a scene over. Not here and not now."

God, she was far more level-headed than he was feeling at the moment, and he appreciated her reeling him in before he did something to ruin his parents' night that he'd regret later. He jammed his fingers through his hair, needing a few minutes to calm the fuck down, preferably without fifty or more guests around.

An idea came to mind. He was going to take Hailey somewhere, a place where they could be alone until he decompressed, and give her the chance to relax away from everyone, as well. Sliding his hand into hers, he guided her back into the house, where it was blessedly quiet.

She followed him past the kitchen and living

room area, probably because he wasn't giving her a choice at the moment. "Max . . . where are we going?"

"You'll see," he replied, not breaking stride as they walked through the foyer and up one of the double staircases to the second floor. He continued down a hallway and stopped at the third door on the left-hand side, which was closed. He twisted the knob, pulled Hailey inside, and shut the door, then switched on one of the lamps on the nightstand to illuminate the space.

She gasped in delighted surprise, and just that one animated sound had the ability to soothe his irritable mood. "Is this your old bedroom?" she asked, taking everything in with wide-eyed charm.

"Yes." It had been years since he'd been in this room, and high school since he'd last brought a girl here. Even for him, it was a total blast from the past. Hell, it still even smelled like the Axe body spray he used back then.

She trailed her fingers over the blue plaid comforter on the queen-sized bed while glancing at the Chicago Cubs posters and banners hanging from the walls, along with other memorabilia and souvenirs he'd collected whenever his father took him and his brother to Wrigley Field to watch a game from one of the private suites located right over home plate.

She looked at the trophies on his dresser and numerous childhood keepsakes, then picked up a framed picture of him in his high school baseball uniform that had been taken his senior year. "What position did you play?" she asked curiously.

He came up behind her, peering at the old photo, and geez, he looked so damned young. "Center field. You know baseball positions?"

"Actually, I do." She set the picture back in its place and turned to face him with a smile. "My uncle was a huge Cubs fan, and I'd watch the games with him all the time, which means I'm a Cubs fan, too."

"My kind of girl." He tapped her playfully on the nose. "We'll have to go to a game together sometime."

"Mmm, we'll see," she said noncommittally as she strolled over to the desk situated in the corner of the room.

He knew she was being a bit guarded, probably because she didn't believe they'd still be together beyond his promise to accompany her to the charity carnival the following weekend.

Especially after what Addison had just said to her, which was undoubtedly still fresh in her mind.

Max already knew he was all in with Hailey, but he also suspected if he brought up a heavy conversation right now about them, she'd most likely be skeptical and end up shutting him out. They had time, and he had patience. As far as he was concerned, both would work to his advantage.

He pushed his hands into the front pockets of his pants, watching as she removed *To Kill A Mockingbird* from his small library of classic books on the shelf above his desk. The novel was creased and dog-eared, and it made him smile when he remembered those late nights before a test when he'd stayed up until morning reading and highlighting passages.

"I read this in high school, too," she said, smiling at the nostalgic memory as she put the book back with the others. "Lit class, right?"

He nodded. "Yep. My mother refused to get rid of any of those classics. She swears that my own kids will probably be required to read them one day, as well."

"She's probably right." She laughed while moving toward a closed door, which she opened, revealing a small walk-in closet.

He reached in front of her and turned on the overhead light. He'd forgotten what was inside, and what he saw definitely made him grin. Clothes and shoes that he hadn't taken to college, and were now clearly dated, hung on the rods. A box labeled baseball cards sat on one of the shelves, and at the far end, his mother had secured his high school letterman's jacket in a clear garment bag to protect it from aging.

"I remember the day I got this jacket and how excited and proud I was to have my varsity letter put on it." Unzipping the bag, he slid the jacket from the sturdy hanger and inhaled the scent of leather, causing him to reminisce about old times. "And my girlfriend at the time wanted to wear it so badly, and I wouldn't let her. In fact, we had a big fight about it, because I told her I didn't want her getting her makeup on it, or to end up having the jacket smelling like her perfume."

He chuckled and shook his head at how ridiculous the argument had been. "I probably could have been more tactful in my word choice, because she totally punished me for being a dick about it."

"Punished you?" Hailey asked, intrigued and amused at the same time. "How?"

He smirked. "She cut me off for two weeks. No sex, no blow jobs, nothing."

Hailey rolled her eyes, though she was grinning. "Oh, yeah, that's quite the harsh punishment."

"I was seventeen years old, and just *looking* at the shape of her breasts beneath her T-shirts made me hard. It was pure torture," he said dramatically. "She didn't give in, not until I finally groveled and apologized, but I still didn't let her wear the jacket. But I'm *much* more mature about it now." He held the jacket open for her and gave her a flirtatious wink. "Want to be the first girl to try it on?"

She nodded eagerly, and the look of pure delight that encompassed her features made his heart do a weird little flip in his chest. It was crazy, but he wanted her to know how special she was, wanted her to *feel* special. She'd told him that she'd never dated in high school, and a part of him wanted her to have this moment, as silly as it might be.

She turned around, and he helped her into the jacket, pulling it up her arms and settling it on her shoulders before turning her to face him again. It was big on her, the sleeves ending at the tips of her fingers and the bottom falling to her thighs. It didn't matter, because she looked fucking adorable. So pretty and sweet and guileless.

In high school, he never would have been mature enough to appreciate a girl like her. As an adult, he realized she was exactly what he'd been waiting for but hadn't known until he'd met her.

He lifted his hands and gently removed her silky hair from the collar so it spilled over her shoulders, then grabbed each side of the jacket and drew her closer, his body warming with need and desire. "You look damn good in my letterman's jacket," he murmured huskily as he dropped his gaze to her mouth.

The soft smile that touched her lips was nothing short of beautiful. "You weren't kidding when you said your bedroom was a time capsule back to when you were a teenager," she said, suddenly engagingly shy. "I kind of feel like *I'm* back in high school and the hottest guy on campus just noticed me."

"I've more than noticed you, sweet girl," he said, and glanced over to the blue paid comforter covering his mattress before waggling his brows at her. "Wanna make out on my bed like two horny teenagers? I promise I'll only go to second base."

"*Only* second base?" She actually sounded disappointed.

"For now," he said as he started walking backward to the bed, pulling her along with him. "But later tonight, when we're back at my place, I'm hoping for a fucking home run."

She laughed, and just as he reached the edge of the mattress, she pressed her hands to his chest and gave him a shove that was so hard and unexpected he lost his balance and fell back onto the bed. He came up on his elbows and cocked his head to the side, suddenly aware of the way she was tugging on her lower lip with her teeth. There was obviously something on her mind, and he waited for her to share what she was thinking.

"There's something I want to show you first," she said, unable to completely conceal the slight nerves he detected in her voice.

Whatever it was, he was certainly intrigued. "Okay."

Her chest rose and fell with a deep, fortifying breath, right before she grabbed the hem of her dress and slowly started raising the material higher and higher. Yeah, he was definitely taken by surprise, but that didn't stop his hungry gaze from automatically lowering to watch as, inch by inch, she exposed her soft, bare thighs, so smooth and supple-looking it took effort not to reach out and slide his hand up the inside of her leg and touch everything she was revealing to him.

It drove him a little crazy, just how much she was teasing him—that she finally felt comfortable enough to do something so intimate when her past experience with the guy in college had destroyed her confidence for so long. He managed to swallow back the ragged, lust-filled groan that rose in his throat, but there was nothing he could do about his rapidly hardening dick and the way it strained against the front of his pants.

When she finally had the material lifted around her hips and he could see the surprise that awaited him, hot desire licked its way straight to his cock. "Oh, fuck me," he muttered appreciatively, absolutely loving what she'd unveiled, for his eyes only. *Light pink cotton panties trimmed in lace.* Most likely the same ones she'd been wearing when he'd asked her if she'd show them to him sometime while she was still wearing them.

The panties were cut a bit higher on the thigh, the pretty lace banded around her hips, and between her legs he could see the faint outline of those soft lips he ached to touch and taste. Practical and innocent-looking, definitely, but they were sexy as fuck on her, and while he'd just promised Hailey he'd only go to second base, he now wanted his hands *inside* those panties.

When he finally lifted his gaze back to hers, the seductive heat in her eyes mesmerized him. "Come here," he said, his tone low and thick.

She neared the bed, and when she was close enough, he reached out and grabbed her, tumbling her onto the mattress beside him. She let out a surprised squeal that turned into a husky laugh, until he moved half on top of her and an instantaneous awareness replaced the playful moment. With one leg pushed in between hers and one of his hands delving into her hair, he lowered his head and kissed her. His lips slid over hers, and his tongue took things deeper, made things hotter and more demanding.

He placed his hand on her leg, right above her knee, and slowly skimmed his palm higher to give her time to adjust to the idea of him touching her intimately. She moaned encouragingly against his mouth, her thighs opening a little wider in invitation as his fingers disappeared beneath the hem of her dress. Just as he neared the sweet spot between her legs, the bedroom door opened behind him and a loud female gasp had Hailey wrenching her mouth from his, then burrowing closer to him in embarrassment, as well as to hide from whomever had just walked in.

Pulling Hailey closer to him and shielding her the best he could with his body, Max glanced over his shoulder and found Addison standing in the doorway, a disdainful look on her face. He narrowed his gaze at her. What the fuck was she doing here? The furious words were on the tip of his tongue, but she spoke first.

"I was looking for the bathroom," she said, her glassy eyes filled with contempt as she shifted her gaze to what she could see of Hailey, which wasn't much.

Max immediately knew it was a lie, that Addison had most likely been looking for the two of them. "Upstairs?" he asked, not bothering to disguise his anger, because yeah, he was still pissed as hell at her for what she'd said to Hailey earlier. "There are *three* of them downstairs."

"They were being used." She shrugged a shoulder insolently.

Yeah, total bullshit. "Well, you missed the bathroom upstairs by two doors down, *before* this bedroom." Which meant she'd already known that herself.

Addison glared at him. "Asshole," she said, her tone vehement.

He almost laughed, because he'd done nothing to provoke this response from her. Clearly, she'd had too much to drink. "Okay, sure, I'll be the asshole," he replied indulgently. "Whatever makes you feel better. Now can you leave?"

She backed out of the room and slammed the door shut behind her. Hailey's body flinched against his, and he exhaled a frustrated stream of breath. Jesus. All he wanted right now was to be alone with Hailey, with no interruptions and a few hours to do all the dirty things to her that he'd been fantasizing about the past week.

It was time to make that happen.

He moved off the bed and held his hand

out to help her up, too. "Come on."

"Where are we going?" she asked once she was standing beside him.

"Back to my place." He gave her a wicked smile as he gently placed his hand on the side of her face and grazed his thumb across her kiss-swollen bottom lip. "That pretty mouth of yours has some begging to do, and I'm ready to hear it."

Chapter Ten

H AILEY FOLLOWED MAX into his Lake
Shore condo, the first time ever that she'd
been at his place. He switched on a light,
providing a glimpse of sleek gray and black
decor with chrome accents, but he didn't take
the time to give her a tour. Instead, he took her
hand and led her down the hallway and into the
master bedroom, which was furnished with a
dark wood dresser and night tables, a comforta-
ble-looking armchair, an oversized ottoman,
and a modern platform bed frame that held a
king-sized mattress.

She wasn't going to lie. The thought of having sex with Max filled her with anticipation and
excitement, but there was no denying the teeny-
tiny touch of worry that still lingered. Revealing

her curvy thighs and panties was one thing. Baring her less-than-perfect body and all its flaws was a whole different situation that took double the confidence to carry out.

But as anxious as she was, in her heart she trusted Max. In the long run, maybe Addison was right and he'd lose interest—that was certainly Hailey's greatest fear, especially when she could already feel her emotions getting involved—but for this moment, she wanted to forget all the drama with Addison, her cruel words, and just enjoy tonight with Max.

He stopped at the foot of the bed and gently tucked a few strands of her hair behind her ear, his concerned gaze searching her features. "Are you nervous?"

She smiled at him and decided to be honest. "It's a little hard not to be, but I want this. I want *you*."

His relief was obvious. "Good, because I want you so fucking badly, and I want tonight to be so damn good for you. I don't want to mess this up."

"I doubt you will." She had the hang-ups and worries, not him.

"I put something in the bathroom for you before I left today to pick you up," he said, glancing toward the adjoining en suite. "I want you to go and put it on."

She had no idea what awaited her, but she was undeniably curious and willing to do as he asked. "Okay."

Once she was inside the spacious bathroom that had a shower big enough to fit a small party in and a large Jacuzzi tub for baths, she found a pale-pink-handled bag on the counter with a black satin bow and the name of the store where it had come from printed across the front. *Agent Provocateur.* A high-end lingerie boutique that she'd driven by many times but never believed they'd have something to accommodate her body type. A Victoria's Secret model she was not.

Tentatively, she removed the bundle of tissue paper inside, not sure what to expect—and hoping to God that it wasn't something so risqué that she'd feel uncomfortable wearing it. But the one thing she was coming to realize about Max was that he understood her insecurities, and he'd never exploit them, so she peeled away the tissue and exhaled a soft breath when she discovered what he'd bought for her—a short slip-type nightgown in black silk chiffon that was trimmed in black French appliqués along the hem and had a low-cut décolletage. There was also a pair of matching silk and lace panties. The ensemble was so pretty, but sexy, too, and she couldn't wait to try it on and wear it for Max.

She stripped out of her current clothes and put on the two pieces, loving the feel of the silk against her skin as the short gown fell into place, then glanced at her reflection in the mirror. *Oh, wow*, was her first thought, because she'd never, ever worn anything so provocative in her entire life or felt so sensual and seductive. The soft fabric outlined the shape of her full breasts yet fit more loosely over her hips as the hemline fell to mid-thigh. Both the slip and panties were modest and demure in terms of coverage, outlining her curves yet leaving everything beneath to the imagination for now, making her feel bold and daring.

She stepped out of the bathroom to find that Max had undressed and was wearing a pair of tight black boxer briefs and nothing else. If she thought he was gorgeous in a suit, his naked body was a work of art, all solid, cut muscle— from his wide shoulders to his defined chest to that ripped abdomen . . . and oh, God, the deep, carved V that she shamelessly followed downward to the substantial bulge confined beneath his snug briefs.

Slowly, he walked in a circle around where she stood, his gaze taking in everything before he stopped in front of her. "Fuck, you look hot."

The compliment made her cheeks warm, in the very best way, because yeah, she *did* feel hot. "How did you know the size?" she asked curiously.

Touching a finger to the lace trim resting at the highest swell of her breast, he leisurely followed the scalloped pattern all the way down to her cleavage. Her nipples automatically puckered against the silk, the fabric rasping against the rigid peaks.

A purely masculine smile curved his lips. "I picked out what I wanted for you to wear tonight, and Natalie helped me with the size since she has a better eye for that sort of thing than I do."

She loved that he'd selected the lingerie himself. "You did good, though I'm sure you paid a small fortune at a place like that."

"Seeing you like this, it was worth every single penny I spent." He lifted his gaze from her aching breasts to her face. "Now let me tell you why I bought this lingerie for you, because there is a specific reason. One, I wanted you to *feel* as beautiful and sexy as you are, and two, wearing this negligee and panties is going to force you to beg for what you want."

Not making the connection, she tipped her head in confusion. "How so?"

"I told you that I'd never pressure you for anything you're not ready to willingly give me, and I meant it," he said, making her realize just how much thought and planning he'd given their first time together. "Nothing comes off your body until you beg me to take it off. I want you with me one hundred percent tonight, mentally and physically. Understand?"

She nodded, consenting to his rules and appreciating the fact that he'd considered her insecurities in his planning, since it enabled her to move at her own pace. Knowing that he didn't expect her to strip naked all at once also served to relax her, something he no doubt knew, so she could better enjoy whatever he intended without stressing and worrying about having to suck in her belly or thinking about the light feathering of stretch marks on her stomach from her weight loss. The lingerie concealed everything she was self-conscious about.

"Good." He took her hand, and instead of guiding her toward the bed, he led her to the armchair and oversized ottoman.

He sat down, and as he pulled her onto his lap so that she was sitting on his bare thighs facing him with her knees on either side of his hips, she realized that this position was her personal fantasy, the one she'd revealed to him that night on the phone when he'd asked her *how do you want to be fucked?*

He placed his warm, strong hands on her knees, his fingers massaging her thighs as he skimmed them beneath the hem of her slip and slowly up her spread legs. "The last time I made you come, it was on the phone and I couldn't watch you climax. I want that tonight. I want to watch as I give you that pleasure."

Oh, yes, please. Those fingers, so close to her center, made her clit throb shamelessly with need. With his hot, dark gaze holding hers, he pressed his thumbs firmly against the silk panel covering her sex, and her breath caught as the wet heat of her arousal seeped through the fabric. She was already wet, her flesh sensitive and slick. He smiled knowingly as he added more of a sliding pressure, which also increased the friction all along her slit and right back up to that central bundle of nerves. His expert touch was exquisite torture.

Her insides quivered, and she grabbed on to his shoulders, her nails digging into his skin as a soft moan escaped her. Her knees clenched tighter against his hips, and she arched against his skillful fingers, her wanton body already chasing the promise of ecstasy he was deliberately dangling just beyond her reach.

She rocked harder against his hand, all to no avail, and a frustrated sound rolled up from her throat. "Max . . . you're teasing me."

"Yeah, I am." An unapologetically devilish grin curved his lips as his thumbs continued to work her over—rubbing, pressing, circling deftly. "Is there something you want, sweet girl? Something you need?"

"I need . . ." Oh, God, how did she say that she needed direct contact to orgasm? "Take my panties off. *Please*," she begged, beyond caring so long as it meant finally getting the release her body craved. "I want you to touch me and kiss me and . . . make me come."

Before she realized his intent, his hands clamped around her waist, and he tipped her backward so that her entire upper body lay on the ottoman, with her hair tousled around her head and her legs over the side. She hardly had time to process what was happening as he grabbed the sides of the lace underwear and yanked it down her limbs, nearly ripping the delicate fabric in his haste to get it off.

Then he dropped to his knees on the floor in front of her. His big palms pushed her legs indecently wide apart so there was no way to hide what he'd just bared to his gaze, and his mouth touched down on the inside of her thigh, hot and damp and beyond erotic. Her body jolted in shock, sending her mind spinning and her heart racing.

"*Max.*" The uncertainty in her voice rang out.

He lifted his head just enough for her to see his sexy smirk and the lust branding his features. "You said you wanted me to kiss you and make you come."

She groaned. She had, but *oh, my God*, that's not what she'd meant at all. She wanted his mouth on her mouth, not on her . . . pussy.

His soft, scorching tongue licked a little higher, and in a panic, she grabbed a fistful of hair to stop him. "No one . . . has ever . . ."

"Let me be the first," he murmured, his voice husky, coaxing, hopeful. "Unless you want me to stop?"

The moment of truth had arrived. Max was a man of his word, and there was no doubt in her mind if she said *stop*, he would, immediately. But now that she was this close, now that *he* was this close, did she really want to refuse something she'd fantasized about for years? Or did she want to experience what the wet heat of Max's mouth would feel like against the sensitive, tingling flesh between her legs?

It didn't take her long to decide.

"Please, don't stop," she whispered, surrendering that part of herself to him.

He groaned, as if she'd given him the greatest gift imaginable, when she knew it was going to be the other way around. "I promise you won't regret that answer," he said in a rasp of voice as he draped her legs over his shoulders.

And then, as if he was afraid she'd change her mind, his mouth was on her in an open, greedy, carnal kiss that made her cry out from the instantaneous shock of pleasure that surged through her. He flattened his palms on her silk-covered stomach, skimming them upward, over her ribs and higher, until he reached her covered breasts. He squeezed the mounds through the material while his tongue swept through her folds, stroked along her cleft, and swirled around her clit once, twice, three times before catching that tender bud between his lips and sucking hard.

She moaned loudly, her desire spiking to an overwhelming level.

He lightly pinched her nipples between his fingers, tugged a little harder, and she felt that twinge of pain all the way down to her pulsing clit. The length of her body shuddered of its own accord, and her hips bucked shamelessly against his mouth, her sex clenching as indescribable sensations converged into a relentless ache at her core.

And now she understood the term *hurts so good*, because every scrape of his sharp thumbnail over her tender nipples was torture. Every hot lash of his tongue across nerve-laden tissues was bliss. Having this man's mouth devour her was beyond anything she ever could have imagined or anything she'd ever experienced. And still, he incited her higher and higher, until she was dizzy and delirious and desperate for release.

"Max, *please*," she implored frantically. Her fingers twisted harder in his hair, not to push him away but to make sure he didn't leave her like this, a hot, wild mess of unfulfilled need.

He didn't disappoint. His mouth and tongue doubled their efforts, and when he pushed two fingers deep inside her, she finally flew apart, the orgasm so intense she heard herself scream until her throat was hoarse. Pleasure suffused every single molecule in her shuddering body. Stars burst across her vision, and finally, a sweet, overwhelming oblivion claimed her.

For a moment, she felt drunk, wonderfully so, and utterly sated. And when her breathing finally evened, her heartbeat slowed, and her mind started working again, she opened her eyes to find Max standing in front of her—while she was still sprawled on the oversized ottoman. He'd removed his boxer briefs, and now he was completely, gloriously, magnificently naked. Her heavy-lidded gaze took in the impressive length of his erection, which he was currently sheathing with a condom, and shockingly, desire stirred all over again in her belly.

Finished with protection, he glanced down at her, looking smug and so damned pleased with himself, and truthfully, after the amazing orgasm he'd just given her, he had every right to be arrogant. Feeling a tad self-conscious, she automatically smoothed the hem of her short slip back down to her thighs—ridiculous, of course, considering where Max had just been and what he'd done, but old habits died hard, and Rome wasn't built in a day.

She smiled up at him, willing to give Max credit for her first oral experience. "Umm, that wasn't half-bad."

"Half-bad?" Chuckling in amusement, he sat down in the chair again, completely comfortable in his nudity. "I guess I'll just have to make sure the *other* half is just as good, if not better." He playfully crooked his finger at her. "Come here, sweet girl. I want you to straddle my lap and ride me."

Ahhh, the other part of her fantasy she'd revealed to him, she thought, as a spark of excitement ignited. She did as he asked, standing up, then situating herself on his thighs so that her sex was only inches away from his cock, which seemed so much bigger and thicker up close and personal. His hands slid up her thighs, pushing the material of her slip up to her hips to expose her pussy to his gaze again, and it was impossible to hold back her moan as he glided both of his thumbs over her still-slick, sensitive flesh.

The lazy smile on his lips belied the banked

hunger in his eyes, telling Hailey that he was exercising great restraint because of her. For her. "That orgasm made you nice and soft and wet," he murmured, his touch between her legs spreading that moisture from clit to core. "You ready to take all of me?"

She nodded eagerly, and he placed his hands on her waist and lifted her up on her knees. "Slide the head of my cock through your pussy to get it good and wet before I fuck you," he ordered huskily.

Shivering at his dirty words, she wrapped her fingers around his length, wishing he weren't wearing a condom so she could feel the heat and hardness of him, skin on skin. As he requested, she rubbed the broad tip through her slippery folds before positioning him at her entrance.

"I'm ready," she whispered.

He locked gazes with her, and with his fingers clutching her hips, he slowly, gradually guided her down onto his shaft. She gasped as the initial pressure of him entering her tight body gave way to a sweet, burning stretch of pain as, inch by inch, he filled her up, until she was completely seated on his cock. He gave her a moment to adjust to the thick feel of him, sliding his hands up her back, then around to cup her breasts in his palms, kneading the flesh through the silk still draped over her body.

"Do whatever feels good," he urged, leaning forward to take one of her breasts into his mouth through the fabric, making her wish the material was gone. "Move as slow as you want or as fast as you need."

Placing her hands on his chest, she rolled her hips against his, moving up and down just enough to feel him gliding inside her, but it wasn't enough to appease the growing ache where they were joined. He bit her nipple, and a sharp mix of pain and pleasure had her whimpering. He instantly soothed it as his tongue curled around the throbbing tip—and God, she desperately wanted to feel his mouth on her bare breasts.

Need overrode any hesitancy, and she slid the thin straps of her slip down her arms until they caught at her elbows, exposing her upper body to his gaze. He groaned at the sight of her breasts but didn't touch them despite how desperate she was for him to. He lifted his eyes to hers; the hunger glimmering in the depths scorched her with a path of fire that shot through her belly and settled between her legs.

"Something you want?" he asked in a low, deep voice that rasped with arousal and his own restraint.

She swallowed hard and nodded. "Your mouth . . . on my breasts . . . sucking my nipples."

As soon as the request left her lips, he fitted his hot mouth over one stunningly sensitive breast. Moaning in relief, she plowed her fingers through his hair and arched her back as his wicked tongue licked and swirled around her taut nipple, as the fine edge of his teeth nipped, overloading her senses and causing her to grind down hard on his cock, seeking to alleviate the tingling in her clit and the throbbing in her core. No matter what she did, no matter how she gyrated against him, it wasn't enough.

She whimpered in frustration. "I need more, Max. Please. So much more."

"I'll give it to you," he promised as one of his hands wrapped her hair tight around his fist, forcing her head back in a way that bowed her body and forced her breasts and nipples to rub against his chest. She couldn't move easily, and it felt as though he were holding her captive— and dare she admit that she liked that bit of control he exerted over her?

Lord help her, she did. Very much.

He flicked his tongue along her throat, his free hand grabbing her ass and lifting her hips a few inches, giving him the last bit of leverage he needed to take over. Without warning, he surged up into her, filling her again and again, so hard and deep, so relentless it stole the breath from her lungs, and all she could do was grip his shoulders and surrender to his sensual assault.

Then his strokes changed, each rhythmic, driving thrust more angled, and oh, God, the head of his shaft dragged repeatedly over an incredibly sensitive spot inside of her that caused her knees to tighten instinctively at his sides. She started to pant as the anticipation built, as the knot in her belly turned to liquid sensation that sizzled along her nerve endings every time he sank into her, every time he withdrew.

"That's it, sweet girl," he growled against her throat, his voice burning with demand and desire. "Feel me. *All* of me."

She did. There was no escaping the way he pummeled into her, and she didn't want to, not when each heated slide of his cock continued to steal her sanity, and another phenomenal orgasm beckoned. He bit the side of her neck, tugged on her scalp a little harder, and she closed her eyes as the waves of passion built, then cried out moments later as an exquisite climax crashed over her.

"Jesus," she barely heard Max swear as her sheath contracted around him, milking him. "You feel so fucking good."

Before her orgasm ebbed completely, he slammed her down onto him, his hand letting go of her hair to grab her hips so he could grind against her pussy, so he could work his shaft deeper inside her as his own release approached at breakneck speed. She opened her eyes in time to watch him, to see him unravel and lose control.

His head was tipped back, the cords in his neck straining, the muscles across his shoulders bunching beneath her hands. His lips parted on a groan as his thrusts grew shorter, faster, more erratic, then his entire body tensed, and shockingly, Hailey felt his shaft pulse deep inside of her as he came, the sublime pleasure on his face thrilling her.

Wow. She'd done this to him. She smiled to herself as the thought drifted through her mind before she gave into exhaustion and collapsed completely against him.

MAX WOKE UP before the alarm went off early the following morning, his happy dick already hard as wood at the feel of a warm, soft, lush body spooned up against him. Not just any body. Hailey's. He was also equally pleased to find that he held a generous handful of breast, and he couldn't resist plucking the firm nipple with his fingers.

Hailey moaned in her sleep but didn't wake up. After the three times he'd fucked her last night, Max knew he should give her the next forty minutes to catch up on her rest before they had to get up. It was Monday, and she needed to be at her office at nine for a client, but he was too fucking selfish to waste the time on dozing, especially now that he'd finally gotten Hailey *completely* naked.

He smiled to himself. Last night's seduction had been a resounding success. The lingerie he'd bought her had proved its worth, giving Hailey the confidence to be a bit daring that first time, and by the second round, he'd managed to coax her out of the slip, too. Baring her body to him hadn't been easy for her, he knew, but he was fairly confident that by the third time he had her writhing beneath him, he'd finally convinced her that her sexy curves turned him on, the proof of which was currently very eager to be buried deep inside of her again. He didn't think he'd conquered every single one of her insecurities, but he was determined that, in time, he would slay them all.

He'd had plenty of short-term relationships over the years, but Hailey was the first woman to make him feel invested in what they could have together beyond this fake engagement. Because after last night, there was no doubt in his mind that he was on the downhill slide of falling in love with her. He wanted *more* with Hailey. He wanted to be her protector and the man she turned to when she needed something. Wanted more fun, playful moments together. More of her smiles and laughter and watching her beautiful face as she came for him while he was deep inside her soft, lush body.

But most of all, he wanted a future with her. The thought of not having her in his life after he fulfilled his end of the bargain next weekend at the charity event was something he didn't even want to consider, and he had that long to convince her that his feelings for her were the real deal. Not an easy feat when he knew how closely she guarded her heart and emotions because of her insecurities that went much deeper than just her body issues.

But right now, before they each went to work for the day, he intended to make sure there was no doubt in her mind just how much he desired her. If that's what he had to build on to show her how much he cared, then that was where he'd start.

As quietly and easily as he could so he didn't wake Hailey yet, he reached over to the nightstand, where there were a few foil packs left unused, and he rolled a condom down his thick shaft. She was lying on her side, the covers tucked beneath her arm, and he gently tugged the comforter and sheet down her body. He almost laughed when she didn't so much as stir. Clearly, he'd exhausted her last night.

It was still fairly dark in his room, and even though his eyes had already adjusted, he knew she'd appreciate the obscurity, and in this instance, he was happy to provide it. Settling on his side behind her again, he trailed his fingers lightly along the indentation of her waist and up the slope of her hip, loving the silky feel of her skin. She sighed, and he continued his exploration. Her top leg was angled away from the bottom one, enabling him to easily glide his fingers through that warm junction between.

She was soft and dewy and inviting, and as he pushed two fingers through her flesh and circled her clit, her hips pushed back against his hand.

Grinning at her response, he buried his face against her neck and hair, inhaling the musky scent of himself on her, along with a touch of everything that made her feminine. It was a fucking heady combination and sent another surge of blood to his excruciatingly stiff cock.

"Hailey," he murmured softly in her ear, gently coaxing her awake with an arousing stroke, not wanting to take her until she was completely aware of what was happening.

Her body stirred a little more, and when he eased two long fingers inside her and deliberately massaged that sensitive patch of flesh just inside her channel, her sensual gasp and the fluttering of her lashes as she opened her eyes told him she was definitely coming around.

"Morning, sweet girl," he said huskily as he trailed kisses along her smooth shoulder while fucking her with his fingers and getting her ready to accept his aching cock.

"Ummm," she hummed, trying to turn around until he stopped her. "I thought I was dreaming."

He chuckled, the sound low and sexy in the dark. "You always have these kinds of erotic dreams?"

"Mostly since meeting you," she admitted, and moaned when he pressed his fingers deeper before dragging them back out to play with her clit. "What time is it?"

He rubbed his stubbled cheek against hers, even knowing she'd most likely end up with beard burn. He liked the idea of marking her. "Almost five thirty, which means I have thirty minutes to introduce you to sleepy morning sex. The perfect way to start a day, in my opinion. And the best part? You get to relax and I'll do all the work, and you'll get an orgasm out of it, too."

"How do you want me?"

"Every fucking way I can have you," he answered automatically, and meant it in more ways that just this physical act. "But right now, I'll take you just like this. Put your legs together and bend your knees forward so they're slightly raised, then tilt your ass back toward me."

She did as he asked, and as soon as she was

in position, he aligned himself along her backside, pressing the head of his dick between her damp petals of flesh that parted as he eased into her from behind. He pushed into her slowly, languidly, filling her up until he was as deep as he could go.

He clasped her hip with one of his hands to keep her from moving. He brought the other around Hailey and gently circled his fingers around her throat right below her chin, then tipped her head back and held it in place so his mouth was at her ear and he was in control. Last night, during their first time together, he'd discovered that Hailey enjoyed when he was more aggressive, more dominant, and her soft moan of acquiescence and the sweet clenching of her pussy around his cock right now told him that she was totally turned on.

He kissed her jaw and rocked his hips against hers, his shaft gliding out to the tip, then all the way back inside the tight clasp of her body again. The slick heat surrounding him, hugging him, felt like motherfucking heaven. Slow and steady, he moved, gradually building momentum, and judging by her soft gasps and low, delirious moans, he knew she was getting close, too.

"Touch yourself," he ordered gruffly, needing to feel her inner muscles squeezing his dick. "Make yourself come."

His sweet, dirty girl obeyed, her hand delving between her thighs, her fingers touching, stroking, faster and faster, matching her rapidly increasing panting breaths. And every time she came into contact with his shaft, that fleeting touch made him a little hotter, a little wilder, a whole lot crazier.

"*Max*," she groaned. The frantic sound of his name on her lips and the way she was pushing her ass back against his hips to take him harder, faster, let him know she was on the cusp, as he was.

Her mouth fell open on a soft cry of pleasure, and she began to shake with the intensity of her climax, while deep inside her body, that rippling sensation enveloped his cock, gripping the length like a tight fist, those internal spasms sending him over the edge with her. A growl tore from his throat as his orgasm blasted through him. He gripped her hip so hard to keep her steady while he drove into her, again and again, that he hoped to God his fingers didn't leave bruises.

When they were both spent and finally coming down from the adrenaline rush, he placed a gentle kiss on her cheek and reluctantly pulled out of her. He went into the bathroom, took care of the condom, and cleaned up, and when he returned, she had the sheet pulled up to her chest. After what she'd just given him, he didn't say a word. It was enough, for now, that she wasn't wearing anything at all.

"I need to get up," she said, her warm, dark eyes all over his body, which he didn't mind a bit. "And you're going to have to drive me back home."

"I will. But first I need a few minutes to re-cover, and then I'm making you breakfast before I take you back," he said as he slid into bed beside her again.

She ran a self-conscious hand through her tousled hair. "You don't have to do that."

He rolled his eyes. "Yes, I know that. I want to, so let me, because it will make me very happy to feed you and know that you're going to work with a full stomach."

He pulled her into his arms and was grateful when she didn't resist and snuggled into his side, her soft, warm body pressing against his. They had a few minutes yet before they really needed to be up and moving, and he wasn't sure when he was going to see her next.

"What's your week like?" he asked, thinking and planning ahead.

She lifted her head from his shoulder, her complexion a rosy pink from her most recent orgasm. "It's pretty busy. I have a few match-making receptions this week in the evenings, four client interviews, and a whole lot of packing to do for the move, both at the office and at home. And you and I have the charity carnival this coming weekend on Saturday."

"I'm looking forward to it. In fact, I meant to tell you that I had Olivia look up Maureen to make a donation to the Mercy Home for Boys & Girls on behalf of Premier Realty."

She smiled at him, her fingers absently sliding down to his abdomen, then back up to his chest, as if she enjoyed just touching him. "Thank you. I'm sure she appreciated that."

She had, and he'd been happy to contribute to a worthy cause. "I was also able to get the guys at the office, and Natalie, to donate their time to help out at the carnival on Saturday. Maureen was thrilled to have the extra help."

Hailey laughed, her blue eyes sparkling. "More like she saw the opportunity to have some hot guys without shirts to sit in the dunking booth so the wealthy ladies will open up their wallets to buy some balls." Her eyes widened. "Oh, my God, that totally sounded dirty."

He chuckled as he pushed his fingers into her hair and gently massaged her scalp. "Yeah, it did. But just for the record, if I'm sitting up on that dunk tank bench, my balls will remain intact, thank you very much."

They both had a busy week, but after last night with Hailey and this morning's revelation, he was determined to make the most of any time he could get with her.

Chapter Eleven

HAILEY SHAMELESSLY WATCHED as Max stripped off his T-shirt, the sun gleaming off of his smooth skin as he revealed his toned chest and the muscled abs that were going to have the women at the carnival raking over cash for a chance to ogle his hot, sexy body before trying to dunk him. Wes, Kyle, and Connor followed suit, until all four of them were standing next to each other in just their jeans, looking like a lineup of gorgeous Chippendale dancers.

"Oh, my God," Brielle muttered beneath her breath so only Hailey could hear. "If I make a donation, can I touch? Maybe lick a little?"

Hailey laughed, though she completely understood her friend's lustful fascination with the men, because all four of them were prime male specimens with amazingly fit bodies. "You can look all you want for free, but no touching, and definitely no licking."

Brielle folded her arms over her chest and feigned a pout. "Killjoy."

While Natalie collected all of their T-shirts, Connor shifted uncomfortably on his feet and glared at Max. "When I agreed to help out today at this carnival, this is *not* what I had in mind, bro. So not cool."

"Suck it up, Connor," Natalie said to her brother, grinning. "Women are objectified all the time."

Hailey glanced at Max, who had his arms crossed over his chest, which only served to accentuate his broad shoulders and firm biceps. "I did warn you that Maureen was going to put you guys on rotation over at the dunking booth." Maureen had taken one look at them and her eyes had lit up. She'd immediately pointed them in the direction of the tanks and dubbed the game "Dunk a Hunk."

"The things we do in the name of charity," Kyle said with a grin that told her he didn't mind being half-naked in the least. Not if it got him extra female attention. Not only was he good-looking but the fact that he had a sleeve of tattoos on his muscled arm would definitely attract women, too.

Maureen came by at that moment with a clipboard in hand, the lanyard around her neck letting everyone know that she was the coordinator for today's charity carnival. She was about the same age as Max's mother, but that didn't stop the other woman from blatantly staring at their chests.

"My goodness," she said, fanning herself with her clipboard. "I know it's a beautiful spring day, but you four are definitely turning up the heat today."

"We're happy to be here and help raise money for the charity any way we can," Max said, charming the pants off Maureen with his comment and his mega-watt smile.

Maureen leaned toward Hailey and said in a low voice, "That man of yours is absolutely swoon-worthy."

Hailey silently agreed, and for the next few days, he *was* hers.

This past week they'd only seen each other sporadically because of their schedules, and the two times they'd had dinner together at his place, she'd tried to bring up the conversation of how this fake engagement was going to end and when. Both times he'd managed to distract her with a kiss that led to the most amazing sex she'd ever had. God, the things that man could do with his hands and mouth were sinful, and he always left her in an orgasm-induced coma for hours afterward . . . with no time to have a serious discussion between them.

But the truth was, as much they were both enjoying this engagement with benefits, from the very beginning, there had been an unspoken end date. The charade couldn't go on forever. And really, after the confrontation with Addison at his parents' house that made it clear Hailey wasn't Max's usual type, she'd known the end was coming.

Add in the fact that Max's mother and sister, and Max himself, had claimed he was a confirmed bachelor, and that merely supported he wasn't looking for anything serious or long term. Once he was put on display today for Maureen's benefit, and after he kept Hailey's credibility intact, the agreement would have served its purpose for both of them.

They could announce a mutual and amicable breakup as soon as next week. She needed to let him know and stick to that decision, because she was beginning to realize that she couldn't keep seeing Max and sleeping with him and pretending all those wonderful feelings were for real. Because for her, their make-believe feelings were no longer an act, something she'd come to acknowledge over the past few days. She'd always been attracted to Max and had spent the past three and a half months getting to know him and the past few weeks falling in love with him.

For the first time in her life, she was in love with a man, and while she wished she could celebrate the emotion and embrace it, she was instead bracing herself for heartache, because their time had, indeed, come to an end. No matter how painful it was going to be to let Max go and revert to being just friends, she knew it was for the best.

She managed to put on a smile for Maureen's benefit. "So, where do you need us girls?"

"I'm going to put you over there in that booth," Maureen said, indicating a covered area with sweets already on display. "You'll be selling the homemade caramel apples, the cotton candy, kettle corn, and wine coolers for adults wearing a red wristband. And you'll also have a great view of your men in the dunk tank," she added with a wink.

Yes, at least they'd have fun watching the guys get soaked. Their section of the carnival was catered more toward the twenty-one-and-older crowd, with adult Twister, wine tasting for a fee, a beer garden, and an area that was roped off for those who wanted to play black jack, poker, or roulette. There were also various vendors selling their wares and food trucks offering different fare.

Maureen checked off a few things on the list attached to her clipboard. "You all have the ten-to-two shift, then I have another group coming in to take over, and you're free to enjoy the carnival yourselves for the rest of the afternoon. I'll check in with you a little while later," she said, then moved on to talk to the volunteers running the casino games.

"I guess I'll see you in a little bit," Max said as he came up to Hailey and kissed her softly on the lips, for Maureen's benefit, no doubt. But when he lifted his head, his gaze was warm and smiling. "By the way, have I told you how pretty you look today?"

She'd dressed comfortably in a white eyelet blouse and jean capris and flats—nothing that truly warranted that heart-stopping look in his eyes, yet she did feel breathless. God, she was going to miss this, how he made her feel so beautiful and happy just to be with him.

"Yes," she managed to say. "When you picked me up earlier."

"Well, it bears repeating, sweet girl," he murmured, for her ears only as he tugged playfully on the tail end of the thick side braid that came over her shoulder and rested right above her breast. "I like what you did with your hair, too. It's kinda fun to pull on the end," he teased huskily.

"What are you, in second grade?" Wes joked, coming up beside Max. "Gotta tug the pretty girl's braid to let her know you like her?"

Max chuckled and let go of her hair. "Yeah, something like that."

"Well, save the hair pulling for later, kids." Wes hooked his finger toward the tanks. "We've got work to do and money to make for charity."

Everyone went to their designated posts, and as soon as Hailey and the two other women arrived at their booth, Natalie claimed the cotton candy machine and Brielle went for the kettle corn, which left Hailey with the caramel apples.

Within the next half an hour, the area was teeming with people, and the three of them were so busy they were only able to watch the guys in the dunk tank at occasional lulls. But there always seemed to be a continuous line, mostly young women wanting to claim bragging rights for dunking a hunk, which wasn't easy to do, Hailey realized as she watched many of the softballs soar right over the bull's-eye arm. At a dollar a throw, the guys were making bank for the charity.

A while later, Max's mom and dad came up to the booth, a pleasant surprise for Hailey since she genuinely liked them both. After issuing the invitation last week at the barbeque to Grace and Kristen, she hadn't been sure if they really would come by, but she was glad they did. Hailey was currently the only one without customers—it seemed that the kettle corn and cotton candy were more popular than the caramel apples—but that enabled Grace and her husband to walk right up to her counter.

Grace greeted her with a warm smile. "It's so good to see you again, Hailey," she said, leaning over the table to give her a hug. "I see that Max and the boys are making excellent use of their good looks and charm over at the dunk tanks."

Hailey laughed. "Yes, they are. The line has been nonstop over there, though they haven't been dunked a whole lot of times. But the women are certainly trying their best."

Douglas glanced across the way to where the boys were, then back again. "It's getting a little warm out. I think I'll go over there and make sure they cool off while Grace gets us each a wine cooler." He winked at Hailey, then sauntered off in their direction.

Hailey withdrew two chilled bottles from the tub of ice behind her, then set them on the counter in front of Grace as she withdrew the money from her wallet to pay. "Thank you so much for coming today," she said, appreciating their support for the charity.

"Of course, dear," Max's mom said, the affection in her voice evident. "You're part of the family, and anything that's important to you is important to us."

A stab of guilt twisted in Hailey's stomach. "Thank you." She truly hated deceiving Max's parents and family, which was another reason for them to put an end to the farce before his mother became anymore attached, too.

"Did Kristen, Alex, and the kids make it?" she asked curiously of Max's sister's and brother's families.

"Yes, we just saw them," Grace said. "They're over at the bounce house trying to get the kids to burn off some excess energy, then they're heading over to the petting zoo."

Hailey smiled, easily imagining those rambunctious nephews of Max's having a blast in the huge inflatable castle. "Sounds like they're having fun."

"They are, and so are we." Grace tipped her head with a smile. "It's such a beautiful day out; I hope you'll be able to enjoy the carnival fun, too."

Hailey added a few more caramel apples to her display to keep it filled. "Actually, we all get off at two and have the rest of the day to ourselves."

"Then why don't we make plans to have a late lunch together?" Grace suggested brightly. "I'm sure by then you'll all be hungry. There's a hamburger place right over that way with picnic-style benches, and I'll save a few of them so we can all sit together."

Hailey couldn't bring herself to say no or make any excuses not to join them. As far as

Max's family was concerned, she was still his fiancée and they were treating her like it. "Sure. That sounds great. I know the boys will be hungry after their shift at the dunk tanks."

A loud buzzer rang out, along with a chorus of cheers on the other side of the section they were in. Hailey glanced up just as Grace turned around, and they both laughed when they realized that Douglas had just dunked Kyle, and with a single throw, he dunked Wes, too. Max and Connor were standing on the sidelines since it wasn't their turn, their chuckles and ribbing adding to the entertainment.

And that's when Hailey saw Addison, standing off to the side by herself, her arms crossed over her chest and her gaze on Max—who hadn't yet seen her. She was wearing a cute strapless dress and sandals, the kind that were turning male heads as they walked by, but she didn't notice any of them. Her stare never wavered from Max. It was, as Max would put it, stalker-ish.

Hailey's stomach churned with unease. On one hand, she couldn't say she was surprised to see Addison. Most likely Max's mother had mentioned the charity carnival to Priscilla, probably even commenting that Max was going to be here helping out, and from there, Hailey had no doubt Priscilla had told Addison. Hailey didn't think for one minute that Addison was there to support the charity, judging by the intense way she was staring at Max.

"We'll see you and the gang at the burger place at two then," Grace said as she picked up the wine coolers, oblivious to what had caught Hailey's attention.

"Yes," Hailey said with a nod. "We'll be there."

Hailey watched as Grace headed off to the dunk tanks to talk to Max and Douglas, and when she shifted her gaze back to Addison, her entire body stiffened when she saw the other woman heading in her direction. She already knew how nasty Addison could be, and she refused to stoop to her level. Killing her with kindness was the best defense Hailey had, so she put on a smile as Addison came up to her table.

At the moment, neither Brielle nor Natalie had any customers, either, and Hailey was grateful that there was no one else around. There was no telling what would come out of Addison's mouth or what was about to go down.

She exhaled a calm breath and ignored the way Addison looked her over with what she could only describe as loathing. "Can I get you something to eat or drink, Addison?" she asked pleasantly.

Addison wrinkled her nose in obvious distaste. "I don't really see anything here that I can eat that won't end up on my hips. You know how that is, don't you, Hailey?" A fake smile that looked more like a sneer lifted her plump, injected lips.

The insinuation was clear, that Hailey had overtly curvy hips compared to Addison's skinny, slender figure. "Actually, yes, I do know how that is," Hailey replied, completely throwing Addison off with her honesty instead of caving to her normal insecurities. There was no denying that she still occasionally indulged, and yes, she had a little padding in places.

Out of the corner of her eye, she could see that Brielle and Natalie had both stopped what they were doing and were looking at Addison with concern. Neither woman knew who she was, but it was clear that they didn't care for what she had to say.

"I'm surprised that they'd trust you around all these sweets," Addison said with a wave of her hand over the caramel apples. "Or did you volunteer so you can spend the day sampling the sweets when no one's around?"

What a bitch, Hailey thought, and it was all she could do to hang on to her composure, but she'd never ruin Maureen's event or make a scene.

"Excuse me," Natalie snapped defensively, taking Hailey by surprise as she moved closer to Hailey's side. "And who are you exactly?"

Addison looked down her nose at Natalie in a condescending manner. "I wasn't talking to you, and I don't think that's any of your business."

Natalie's shoulders straightened and her gaze narrowed on Addison. "Oh, yes, it *is* my business when you're talking shit to my friend."

Wow, Hailey admired Natalie's gutsiness, and while she appreciated the other woman's support, she knew how ugly this whole scenario with Addison could get. She put her hand on her friend's arm. "Natalie, I'm okay, really. I'll explain everything later."

But Addison wasn't done, and she spewed more spiteful words. "I really can't figure out what Max sees in you, and believe me, I've tried. He can do so much better. Hell, he had better, and then a few weeks later, he ends up engaged to you." Addison's gaze dropped to Hailey's stomach, then lifted back up to her face. "Are you pregnant and trapping him into marriage? It's the only thing that makes sense, though I don't understand why he'd sleep with you in the first place."

"Addison, that's low, even for you," Hailey muttered.

"Who the hell *are* you?" Natalie all but yelled, her tone furious, and Hailey had to tighten her grip on her friend's arm for fear she'd leap over the table to have it out with the other woman on Hailey's behalf.

Addison looked completely unfazed, narcissist that she was. "I'm a very good friend of Max's."

Natalie laughed, but the sound was caustic. "I'm going to have to call *bullshit* on that, because I know Max *very* well and he would not be friends, or anything else for that matter, with someone like you."

Hailey was about to put an end to the verbal exchange between the two before the situation escalated just as Maureen came by with her clipboard to check on things, as she'd been doing every hour.

"How are you girls doing?" she asked brightly. "Do I need to send a runner over with anything? More ice or sugar for the cotton candy?"

Brielle shook her head, though her expression still reflected a bit of shock at what she'd just witnessed with Addison. "We just had someone come by, so we're good for now."

Maureen wrote a note on her clipboard, then smiled at Addison. "Are you having a good time?" she asked, automatically assuming she was a visitor at the carnival.

Right before Hailey's eyes, everything about Addison changed . . . from rude and condescending to pleasant and cordial as she smiled at Maureen with such sweetness that it made Hailey nauseous. Obviously, this was the side of her that Max's mother had seen and what had convinced Grace to set her up with Max. She appeared friendly and approachable, but it was all a lie.

"Yes, I'm having a wonderful time," Addison said, addressing Maureen with a delighted smile. "I'm a very good friend of Max Sterling and his fiancée here and wanted to come out and support such a great cause."

Hailey's jaw nearly hit the ground in shock.

Beside her, she could feel the anger vibrating off Natalie, but Hailey was grateful she didn't say a word.

"I couldn't be happier for Max and Hailey," Maureen said, beaming at Hailey and at the same time shaking a chastising finger at her. "Hailey has been keeping Max to herself for too long, and I'm so pleased he was able to finally be here at an event with her."

Addison cocked her head inquisitively. "So, you've known them awhile, then?"

Hailey could hear the slight skepticism in Addison's voice, just enough to tell Hailey that the other woman was suddenly very interested in discovering the details and time frame of their relationship.

"Well, I've known Hailey for quite some time," Maureen replied. "She matched up my son with the love of his life. But I just recently met Max a little over two weeks ago."

"Interesting," was Addison's only response, but her voice was suddenly low and cold.

"Well, I need to move on and check on the other booths," Maureen said, and then she was gone, leaving Addison staring at Hailey with a hateful sneer.

"Definitely interesting," was all Addison

added as she turned and walked away, leaving Hailey with a horrible sense of dread tightening her chest.

"Jesus Christ!" Natalie said, her voice furious. "What a piece of work! There is no way that Max would date someone like that. No freaking way."

"He did, for a while," Hailey confirmed. "Which is part of the reason he agreed to the fake engagement, because she was being so persistent and he wasn't interested."

Natalie shook her head. "Max is going to be *pissed* that she confronted you like that and said those awful things to you."

And that was the last thing Hailey wanted, especially when there was still the issue of Addison being the daughter of Max's father's biggest client. She did not want Max to do anything that would hurt that important business relationship.

"Please don't say anything to Max," Hailey said, unable to hide the plea in her tone. Hopefully, Addison was long gone for now.

"He has a right to know," Brielle said, her voice soft with concern.

"I agree, but I'll tell him later tonight." When they were alone and they could finally discuss the end to their fake engagement.

✧   ✧   ✧

AT TWO O'CLOCK in the afternoon, the next shift for the dunk tank came in to relieve Max and his friends. They all put their dry T-shirts back on, but there wasn't much they could do about their damp jeans for now except let them dry on their own. None of them had thought ahead to bring a change of clothes.

From across the way, he watched as Hailey, Brielle, and Natalie headed in their direction, since their shift was over, as well. He smiled at Hailey as the trio neared, and while she returned the gesture, it seemed forced. Over the past few weeks, he'd learned to gauge Hailey's expressions and moods, and something was definitely off.

When the women were finally at the dunk tank, Wes caught Natalie around the waist and pulled her close. "I'll give a hundred bucks to charity right now if you'll get up on that bench and let me throw just one ball at the bull's-eye."

Natalie pursed her lips, clearly not on board with the idea but torn since her fiancé had just offered a nice sum of money to the charity. "This kind of feels like blackmail," she said unhappily. "How can I say no to charity without looking like a total diva?"

"Umm, you can't?" Connor chimed in, laughing.

Natalie glared at Wes. "You are such a jerk for making me do this, but fine, I'll get up on that bench for the sake of charity," she said, pushing out of his arms.

Wes smacked Natalie on the ass as she started toward the dunk tank. "You know how much I like you wet, baby." He smirked.

"Jesus, Sinclair, there are kids around," Max said, shaking his head incredulously.

Wes ducked his head sheepishly. "Oh, yeah, sorry about that. But it's true."

Max grabbed Hailey's hand and pulled her off to the side as everyone else went back to the water tank to watch Wes dunk Natalie for a donation to charity. He gave the end of her braid a flirtatious tug, and even though she smiled up at him, it wasn't the normal happy expression he'd become so used to seeing.

"Everything okay?" he asked.

She nodded. "I'm just a little tired," she replied, and her reasoning made sense considering how busy she'd been in her booth. "By the way, your parents would like all of us to meet them for a late lunch over at the hamburger place."

"That sounds really good. I'm starved and I'm sure the guys are hungry, too. We'll head over there just as soon as Wes has his fun with Natalie."

Hailey laughed. "Thank you for not daring me to get up on that bench."

He shook his head as he led her back to the group. "That's totally *their* thing, not ours. I don't feel the need to one-up you in any way whatsoever."

All Wes purchased was one softball, and that's all it took to hit the bull's-eye and knock Natalie into the huge tank of water. She landed with a splash and came up sputtering, her hair a wet mess around her face.

"There, are you happy now?" Natalie shouted to Wes as she dried off with a towel an attendant handed to her.

Wes grinned at her, though he gently pushed the damp strands away from her face. "Yes, very happy, Minx."

"Hey, everyone," Max announced. "Let's go get some burgers to eat."

Everyone agreed, and they made their way over to the food section, where Max's family was already waiting for them. They'd claimed two of the tables, and once all the food was ordered and delivered, Max sat down next to Hailey at the table where his parents and siblings were with their kids, while his friends took the table next to them.

His mom and dad were seated across from him and Hailey, with his sister and brother and kids at the far end. His parents told him that they'd enjoyed a bit of the gambling at the casino, and as they all ate their burgers and fries, Max couldn't help but notice that Hailey had only taken a few bites of hers. She seemed distracted, but he'd just have to wait until they were alone to figure out what was really on her mind.

Just as everyone was finishing their lunch and discussing what they wanted to do next, Max glanced up and did a double take when he saw Addison walking toward their table, a smug look on her face that immediately put him on guard. He hadn't even been aware that she was here at the carnival, and judging by the surprised look on his mother's face, she hadn't known, either. But a quick look at Hailey and those big blue eyes filling with unmistakable dread, coupled with her current mood, and there was no doubt in his mind that she'd already seen or talked to Addison today.

She stopped at their end of the table and smiled at his parents. "Hi, Mr. and Mrs. Sterling," she said, so friendly and polite.

"Addison!" his mother said with a smile. "I didn't realize you were going to be here today. Did your mother come with you?"

Addison shook her head. "No, this really isn't her kind of thing, but of course, I wanted to stop by and support the charity," she said, which Max suspected was total bullshit. "And I met Maureen, the lovely coordinator of the event. She and I just had a very enlightening conversation."

With that one statement, Max knew exactly where this conversation was heading and what was about to unfold in front of his family. Beside him, Hailey was tense, but he laid his hand on her knee beneath the table, letting her silently know that, whatever happened, he'd handle it.

"Really?" His sweet, guileless mother had no clue and walked right into Addison's trap. "And what was that?"

Addison flipped her long, straight blonde hair over her shoulder, a perplexed expression on her face. "Well, it seems there's a bit of confusion around Max and Hailey's engagement. We all were told it happened very quickly and within the past few weeks, but Maureen is *insistent* that Max and Hailey have been engaged for well over three months."

His mother frowned, and the rest of his family grew quiet as they listened in, as well. "Well, that can't be true."

Addison nodded her agreement. "You know, that's exactly what I thought, because just a little over a month ago, Max was single and dating *me*. So how could he be engaged to someone else?" Her gaze shifted to Hailey, the too innocent look in her eyes changing to something far more cruel. "Hailey, maybe you can explain what's going on?"

Fuck. Max's jaw clenched tight and it was all he could do to keep a rein on his anger as he met the other woman's gaze head on. "Addison, I don't know what you're trying to prove, but—"

"No, stop, Max," Hailey said, abruptly cutting him off. "The engagement isn't real," she blurted out as she stood, her voice hoarse and her eyes filled with a sheen of tears. "*None* of it is real and it's my fault. I perpetuated the whole thing because I was building my business, and what kind of matchmaker doesn't have her own guy? Max stepped up to help me. None of this was his idea, and I never meant to put anything over on his family. Things just got so out of hand. I'm so sorry if I hurt anyone," she rambled, then quickly stepped over the bench they'd been sitting on and rushed toward the carnival exit.

"Hailey, wait," Max called out, but she didn't slow down. At the table next to theirs, both Brielle and Natalie jumped up and followed Hailey, which was the only thing that kept Max from going after her himself, while his family was staring at him in varying degrees of shock, and Addison stood with a smug look on her plastic face.

Max blew out a rough breath. Okay, he'd deal with his family first, give Hailey time to calm down, and then go make sure she was okay.

"Max, why would you do such a thing?" his mother demanded, her tone laced with disappointment.

Addison crossed her arms over her chest, looking completely vindicated. "Yes, Max, why would you fake an engagement to *her* when you had me?"

Was she fucking kidding him? "It started as a

fake engagement *because* of you," he said, done holding everything back. "Because no matter how many times I nicely and politely told you that I wasn't interested, you couldn't take no for an answer. But obviously you don't know the meaning of the words *polite* or *nice*."

His mother sucked in a surprised breath, her gaze shifting from Max to Addison and back again.

Addison glared at him. "It's so sad that someone who matches couples for a living can't even get herself a boyfriend on her own. I wonder how her clients are going to feel about this little scandal."

Max narrowed his gaze at the evil woman standing in front of him, his hands curling into fists at his sides in pure anger. "You say a goddamn word to malign her character and I guarantee you'll regret it."

"Max!" his mother admonished, clearly appalled to hear her normally polite son threaten someone, but he was beyond worrying about being civilized.

"No, mom, I'm not going to let Addison hurt Hailey any more than she already has," he said adamantly, then glanced at his entire family. "Yes, this started as a fake engagement, but I genuinely care for Hailey. Hell, I fucking *love* her."

Addison gasped, and his mother's eyes got as round as saucers. Beside her, Max saw his sister smirk in a way that told him she was totally impressed with his declaration, and she was giving him her silent blessing.

"That can't be possible," Addison said, her tone incredulous.

"It *is* possible," he said to the bitter, spiteful and clearly delusional woman. "And I don't expect you to understand true love because you can't see anything beyond your own self-interest and hate."

Everyone was silent, until his father finally let out a huff of breath. "Well, son, if you love Hailey, I suggest you go and tell her."

Max almost laughed at his father's response, so straightforward and to the point. "I plan to," he said, then spun on his heel and headed in the direction he'd last seen Hailey run in.

By the time he'd caught up with the three girls, they were already at the parking area. "Hailey, wait," he said, loud enough for her to hear. Despite her obvious need to leave, he wasn't letting her go until she heard what he had to say. Until she knew exactly how he felt about her.

To his relief, she stopped and turned around, the devastated look on her face nearly gutting him.

"Give me a few minutes to talk to you. Please," he said, imploring her to give him a chance.

Hailey said something to Brielle and Natalie, and while the two women walked away to give them some time alone, they didn't go far and could probably hear their conversation. At this point, he'd take whatever he could get.

He closed the last bit of distance between himself and Hailey, and as soon as he reached her, she spoke before he could.

"I'm so sorry—"

"Stop right there," he said, cutting her off. "You don't have a damn thing to apologize for."

She laughed but the sound lacked any humor. "How can you say that after what just happened in front of your family with Addison? We always knew this fake engagement was going to end at some point, but never like that," she said, her voice rough with emotion, even as he saw her defenses rising. "Never in a way that would hurt your parents, who've been nothing but kind to me and don't deserve to be duped. They probably think I'm some desperate woman trying to manipulate their son into a relationship, and I'm sure my credibility as a match-maker is ruined, which truthfully, is my own damn fault."

"First of all, we *both* agreed to this fake engagement, so I refuse to let you take all the blame," he said, hating that she was already putting her guard up and pushing him out, which meant he needed to put everything out on the table. Go broke or go home. "And most importantly, I'm not ready for this, *for us*, to end. I love you."

Her eyes widened in shock, then filled with a wealth of insecurities as she took a cautious step back. "You can't," she whispered in disbelief.

"I can and I do," he said, aching to take her in his arms and hold her tight until she accepted the truth about how he felt. "There is nothing you can say or do that will make me feel any differently, Hailey. Nothing."

He could plainly see all the *what ifs* swirling in her gaze, the doubts and uncertainties that had ruled her life for so long that those ingrained fears were second nature to her. Her resistance was a difficult battle to fight, and in the end, only she could change the ending to their story. Not him.

He braced his hands on his hips and hoped to God he was doing the right thing. "I'm not the kind of guy who walks away or gives up without a fight, Hailey. And I'm not leaving you now, either. But I am going to let you go home so you have time to think about everything we've shared together the past few weeks, and to realize that when I say I love you, I mean it, because I don't say things I don't mean and you should know that about me by now. When you believe it, when you're ready to *let me* love you, I'll be waiting for you and you know where to find me."

Her eyes shimmered with tears and pain, and it was excruciating for Max to turn around and walk away, to give Hailey the time to process everything with a clear head, just as he'd promised.

Whatever happened next was up to her.

Chapter Twelve

HAILEY METHODICALLY PACKED up her office, going through the motions but feeling empty inside. She should have been over-the-top excited that she was signing the closing papers for the Logan Square property this afternoon at Max's office, but instead her stomach was in knots about seeing him again.

A week had passed since that awful day at the carnival with Addison. A week since Max had told Hailey he loved her, and left her standing in the parking lot, torn between wanting to call him back, and letting him go. In the end, her insecurities had won the battle, because cutting Max loose now was far less painful than it happening weeks or months down the road—all because she believed she'd never be enough for a man like Max. That one day, he'd realize that, too, and her heart would never recover from the rejection.

Except her heart already felt shattered, and she was coming to realize that it was *her* doing, not his. She was so concerned about protecting herself and her heart and her emotions, that she'd yet again deliberately sabotaged another relationship. Except this one meant everything to her.

Each day apart from Max didn't ease the ache like she'd hoped. No, it was starting to feel like a huge desolate hole in her chest, and as though an integral part of her was missing and she was lost without that essential piece.

She missed seeing him. Talking to him. Laughing with him. She missed his sexy texts and how he so effortlessly made her feel special and beautiful—always. Not out of obligation, but because he was the kind of man who meant what he said, and what he did—and had proved that statement from the very beginning, time and again. What man went through that kind of effort if what he felt wasn't real?

She'd made such a mess of things in so many ways, and had hurt people she hadn't intended to. She was certain her business was going to take a hit when and if her fake engagement went public, as Addison had threatened. But so far, that hadn't happened, and she was grateful. But she had called Maureen to apologize and to explain why she'd fabricated the whole fake engagement pretense. There really was no excuse for the deception and she should have come clean the moment Maureen had called Max out as her fiancé that day at lunch. The other woman had been surprisingly understanding, though at the end of their conversation she'd made the comment that for a relationship that was supposedly all an act, Max certainly had seemed genuinely taken with her.

Not just taken with her, *he loved her*. God, those words caused both pleasure and pain, and she absently rubbed at the left side of her chest to ease the ache inside. Not for the first time, she questioned her decision to let him go, because there was no doubt in her mind that she'd fallen in love with him, too.

When you believe it, when you're ready to let me love you, I'll be waiting for you and you know where to find me.

More than anyone, she trusted Max. He'd never given her any reason not to, and she realized that she had one of two choices to make. She could cling to the fears and insecurities that had paralyzed her for most of her adult life and be miserable and lonely, or she could be brave and fearless and confront all those doubts that had stolen so much from her already.

One thing she knew for certain, this relationship was different. *Max* was different. In the past, she'd pushed men away before things turned serious in order to protect herself, and every single guy had let her go without even so much as a fight, leading her to believe she wasn't worth the effort. But despite her many hang ups, there was nothing that Max hadn't been able to handle. He'd conquered so many of her doubts, had given her the confidence to believe in herself . . . because she *was* worth the effort—something she needed to believe, too.

And ultimately, that day at the carnival, he'd made himself vulnerable by laying himself bare emotionally, confessing his feelings, and risking *her* rejection.

And that's exactly what she'd done to Max. She'd let him believe she didn't want him, that he wasn't worth the effort, or important enough to fight for. After a week apart, was she too late to change all that?

"Hailey, someone is here to see you," Brielle said, startling her out of her thoughts as she came into her office.

Hailey turned around from the book shelf she was clearing off, a tiny spark of hope flickering inside her. She had no client appointments scheduled for the rest of the day, and there was only one person she wanted to see right now.

"Max?" she asked, speaking the name out loud.

The look that Brielle gave her was to the point. "No. That's up to *you*, remember?"

Hailey winced at her friend's direct reply, but it wasn't anything she didn't already know, or that Brielle hadn't already said before. Many times. Any change had to come from Hailey, and while she was afraid and nervous that Max might have given up on her after a week of silence, she was coming to realize that their relationship was worth risking her heart.

"I'll send the person in," Brielle said without giving a name, then she was gone.

A few second later Max's mother, Grace, walked into her office, and Hailey's initial shock was followed by a dozen different thoughts scrambling through her mind. After the scene with Addison at the carnival, and her fake engagement to Max being exposed to his family, she had no idea where she stood with the woman now standing across the desk from her, and Grace's carefully composed expression didn't give her a clue, either.

"Mrs. Sterling," Hailey said, greeting her politely. "How are you?"

"I'm good, dear. My son, not so much," she said, the hint of sadness in her voice genuine and real. "And didn't we agree you'd call me Grace?"

Hailey nodded, but she was immediately concerned about Grace's insinuation that her son wasn't doing well. "Is Max okay?"

A faint smile touched Grace's lips as she sat down in one of the chairs in front of Hailey's desk. "Physically, Max is absolutely fine," Grace assured her. "But emotionally? I've never seen him so upset and unhappy."

Knowing that she was the direct cause of Max's misery made Hailey's chest ache. "I'm so sorry. I never meant to hurt him."

"The only thing hurting him right now is the possibility that he's lost you for good," Grace said, surprising Hailey with her reply. "And I'm here because I want to make sure that doesn't happen, because despite the fact that the two of you perpetuated a fake engagement, I saw for myself at my husband's birthday party just how much Max cares about you. And now, having seen him this past week, I know without a doubt he loves you."

Hailey slowly sank down into her own chair, and went to turn the engagement ring on her finger, only to remember that she'd taken it off a week ago. "You're not angry that we . . . lied?"

"Well, it was definitely a shock to find out the engagement wasn't real, but I understand why Max did it. I had no idea Addison was so . . . *persistent*," she said, and Hailey knew Grace was trying to be diplomatic about the other woman's personality.

"About Addison, I apologize if this whole situation caused any kind of problems between Douglas and Addison's father," Hailey said, because that was something she'd worried about this past week, too. "I know he's an important client, and Max was concerned that it might hurt their working relationship."

Grace shook her head. "When it comes to business, men don't react on an emotional level like women do. Douglas has already reassured me that nothing has changed in his relationship with Tate Brooks. As for Priscilla and myself, well, things are a bit strained because of course she's going to side with her daughter in all this, but I honestly don't need that kind of drama in my life."

Hailey smiled for the first time since Grace had walked into her office, her own relief palpable.

"I should have listened to Max when he told me he wasn't interested in Addison, but all I wanted was for my son to be happy and settled with a woman who loves him as much as he loves her."

"I do love him," Hailey said, the words absolutely true.

Grace smiled, an insightful twinkle in her eyes. "I know you do, and that's why I'm here. Because the two of you belong together, and it would be a shame for Max to lose the best thing that's ever happened to him."

An overwhelming sense of gratitude filled Hailey. Max had an incredible mother, both parents were wonderful, and it really helped to know his family didn't hold the whole situation against her. Now all she had to do was figure out a way to let Max know she loved him too.

✧   ✧   ✧

HAILEY ARRIVED FIFTEEN minutes early for her appointment at Premier Realty to sign her loan documents, hoping to get a few moments alone with Max before everything shifted to business.

Hailey stopped at Olivia's desk and smiled at the other woman. "Hi, Olivia. I know I'm early for my meeting, but I was hoping to see Max first, if possible?"

"Oh." Olivia's gaze shifted to the phone on her desk. "Looks like he's on a call right now, but I can get you seated in the conference room and let him know you're here and would like to speak to him before the appointment."

"That would be great. Thank you."

She followed Max's secretary to the spacious room and seated herself at the table. With every minute that ticked by, the nerves in her belly increased and she started to overthink the entire situation with Max. What if Olivia told him that Hailey was waiting to talk to him and he wasn't interested? What if Max changed his mind and decided that she wasn't worth the effort? What if . . .

She abruptly shut down her depressing train of thought, because she refused to believe that Max would give up on her after only a week's time. He'd told her that day at the carnival that there wasn't anything she could say or do to make him feel any differently about her, and ultimately she trusted that Max was a man of his word. But knowing that didn't make it any easier to sit and wait for him to arrive.

Unfortunately, the escrow officer showed up first, killing any chance that Hailey might have had to speak to Max alone. Max walked in a few moments later. He greeted both of them with a courteous smile, then settled into a chair besides Hailey.

For the next hour, the escrow officer presented her with so much paperwork it made her head spin, and she was grateful that Max was there to explain things more thoroughly before she signed each document. From the tone of his voice, to his mannerisms, to his body language, everything was impersonal and businesslike and straightforward, as if Hailey was just another client and this was just another sale. By the time she finished, her stomach hurt as did her heart.

When it was finally over, the escrow officer shook her hand and told Hailey it typically took a couple of days for the loan to be funded after the signed paperwork was returned to the lender, but if everything went smoothly, she'd have the keys for the Logan Square property in her hand by the end of the week.

Once they were alone, Max turned toward her with a smile she couldn't quite decipher, but there was no mistaking the weary, tired expression on his face. As if he hadn't slept well the past week, and she understood the feeling. But despite all that, he was still gorgeous and the one man who gave her so much hope for the future. For *their* future together.

"I suppose congratulations are in order," he said, his dark hazel eyes searching hers as he pushed his hands into the front pockets of his pants.

"Thank you," she said, and closed the door to the conference room before he could escape and she lost both her nerve, and her chance, to make this man hers.

Then again, she already knew that she was prepared to fight for him, *for them*, as long and as hard as it took. She was done doubting herself, done questioning if she had what it took to keep a man like Max interested. He'd already proven, more than once, how he felt about her, that he wanted *her*. The proverbial ball was in her court.

The first words that came to mind were *I'm sorry*, but she'd been saying that an awful lot lately, and she knew it was time to get past the hurt and blame and say something much more significant and meaningful. Something that would leave no doubt in his mind that she wanted a future with him.

She leaned against the back of the door and looked him in the eyes, her heart expanding with so much emotion she didn't know how to contain it all.

And so, she didn't. "I love you, Max Sterling."

The corner of his mouth twitched, and his head tipped to the side, the faintest hint of humor replacing the uncertainties she'd seen in *his* gaze. "Are you absolutely *sure* about that, Ms. Ellison? Because I've been waiting an entire fucking week to hear you say those words, and now that you have, I'm not going to let you take them back."

She bit her bottom lip, and shook her head. "I don't want them back. I want you. Forever. It just took me a little longer to trust in the emotion."

With an audible groan, he closed the distance between them, pulled her into his arms, and kissed her so long and hard and deep that by the time he lifted his head again she was dizzy and breathless and unbelievably happy.

He cupped her face in his hands, his thumbs stroking gently over her cheeks, so intimately, so tenderly. "Don't you ever doubt me again, because next time, I won't hesitate to take you over my knee and spank your ass until you believe how much I love you. *All* of you. Got that?"

She nodded and laughed, her heart floating in the clouds as she realized that she loved being in love. With Max. Forever.

Epilogue

Three months later . . .

MAX WATCHED HAILEY mingle with all the guests and clients she'd invited to her open house reception for the new Ellison Agency office. It had taken her three months to get moved in and settled, as well as to decorate and furnish the first two floors of the building to reflect a modern, upscale atmosphere for her match-making business. Judging by everyone's reaction, all her hard work had paid off.

He caught sight of his mother and father talking to Maureen, who was there to support Hailey, as well, even after everything that had happened at the carnival. Then again, he and Hailey were still a couple, just without an engagement ring on her finger. They'd taken the time to date, to spend quality time together alone, and with his family and their friends. If he thought he loved Hailey three months ago, his feelings for her now were so entrenched he couldn't imagine spending the rest of his life without her in it.

As she talked to a client and smiled at something they said, he couldn't help but think how beautiful she was. How radiant and sweet and kind, not to mention as sexy as hell in that black, form-fitting dress he'd coaxed her to wear tonight. It hugged her curves in all the right places, and with her long, gorgeous blonde hair falling around her back and shoulders in soft waves, she was stunning. And when he'd told her that earlier, the best part was, she'd believed him, he thought with a smile.

"What is with that goofy grin on your face?" Wes asked as he came up beside Max, then followed his line of vision to where Hailey had moved on to chat with Brielle and Natalie. "Ahhh, now it all makes sense. When are you going to put a fucking ring on it already?"

Max pushed his hand into the front pocket of his pants, his fingers closing around the small square box he'd put there when Hailey wasn't around. "Soon," he said, beyond ready to make it happen. "Very soon."

Another hour went by as guests enjoyed drinks and hors d'oeuvres, and Max decided he'd had enough of sharing Hailey for a while. He found her with his parents, laughing at something his father said, and Jesus, he didn't think he'd ever get tired of hearing that sound . . . or watching the way her lips softened into a smile whenever she saw him, like right now as he approached the trio.

"I haven't had any time with Hailey, and I'm here to steal her away for a little while," he said, grabbing her hand in his, then sneaking up the back elevator with her to the third floor apartment she now lived in, and where they'd both gotten ready for the party earlier.

"What are we doing up here?" she asked curiously as she followed him into her bedroom.

Releasing her hand, he faced her as she looked up at him expectantly. He always thought that he'd be nervous when he proposed to the woman he loved, but this moment felt so perfect and right there was no room for any other emotion but the love filling his heart to overflowing.

"There's something very important I need

to ask you," he said, very seriously.

Her eyes widened. "Okay," she said quietly.

After reaching into his pocket and retrieving the box, he got down on one knee and popped open the lid, revealing a diamond solitaire ring surrounded by a dozen other sparkling stones. She gasped, her eyes flying to his in disbelief.

"I wanted to do this whole engagement thing properly this time," he teased. "Hailey Ellison, I love you like crazy and I want you to always be mine. Will you marry me, sweet girl?"

"Oh my God," she said, as happy tears filled her eyes. "Yes. Of course I'll marry you!"

He grinned and slipped the ring on the finger that had been bare for too long, then stood up. She jumped into his arms, knocking him backward onto the bed and her on top of him. They bounced on the mattress with both of them laughing, until she sat up, straddling him uninhibitedly, and gazed at the diamond on her finger.

"It's beautiful," she murmured in awe.

"*You're* beautiful," he replied, placing his hands on her knees then pushing his palms beneath the hem of her dress. "And so hot and sexy I'm not letting you go back down to the party until I fuck you."

"I have guest and clients waiting for me!" she said on a squeal of laughter as he tumbled her onto her back. "I can't go back looking . . ."

"Like you just got well and truly fucked by your fiancé?" His fingers reached the sexy lace panties she'd started wearing for him, and all it took was one well placed stroke to make her melt and change her mind.

They didn't make it back down to the party for a good long while.

Thank you for reading FAKING IT. We hope you enjoyed Max and Hailey's story! We would appreciate it if you would help others enjoy this book by leaving a review at your preferred e-tailer. Thank you!

Up next, Kyle Coleman in WELL BUILT.

Order WELL BUILT today!

Sign up for Carly Phillips & Erika Wilde's Newsletters:

Carly's Newsletter
http://smarturl.it/CarlysNewsletter

Erika's Newsletter
http://smarturl.it/ErikaWildeNewsletter

ABOUT THE AUTHORS

CARLY PHILLIPS

Carly Phillips is the *N.Y. Times* and *USA Today* Bestselling Author of over 50 sexy contemporary romance novels featuring hot men, strong women and the emotionally compelling stories her readers have come to expect and love. Carly is happily married to her college sweetheart, the mother of two nearly adult daughters and three crazy dogs (two wheaten terriers and one mutant Havanese) who star on her Facebook Fan Page and website. Carly loves social media and is always around to interact with her readers. You can find out more about Carly at www.carlyphillips.com.

ERIKA WILDE

Erika Wilde is the author of the sexy Marriage Diaries series and The Players Club series. She lives in Oregon with her husband and two daughters, and when she's not writing you can find her exploring the beautiful Pacific Northwest. For more information on her upcoming releases, please visit website at www.erikawilde.com.

Made in the USA
Middletown, DE
21 April 2017